The Author

LEONARD COHEN was born in Montreal, Quebec, in 1934. He received his B.A. (1955) from McGill University and pursued graduate studies in English at Columbia University. Soon thereafter, he returned to Montreal and worked in his family's clothing business while he continued to write poetry.

The year after he graduated from McGill, Cohen published his first volume of poetry, *Let Us Compare Mythologies*, where he brought together his Jewish heritage with classical and Christian myths in lyrical poems that juxtapose religion with sensuality. Although later volumes would adopt a darker, more ironic tone, his poetry continues to explore the individual's quest for love and spiritual transcendence.

In 1961 Cohen left for England, where he wrote his first novel, *The Favourite Game* (1963), a semi-autobiographical account of a Montreal Jewish boy's discovery of his vocation as a poet. During the sixties he achieved national and international acclaim as a composer-singer.

Cohen has lived intermittently in England, on the Greek Island of Hydra, in California, and in New York, although he frequently returns to Montreal, which he still considers to be home.

THE NEW CANADIAN LIBRARY

General Editor: David Staines

Leonard Cohen

THE
FAVOURITE
GAME

With an Afterword by Paul Quarrington

M&S

Library and Archives Canada Cataloguing in Publication

Cohen, Leonard, 1934-
The favourite game

(New Canadian library)
Includes bibliographic references.
ISBN 0-7710-9954-1

I. Title.   II. Series

PS8505.022F38 1994   C813'.52   C89-093676-5
PR9199.3.C65F38 1994

We acknowledge the financial support of the Government of Canada through the Book Publishing Industry Development Program and that of the Government of Ontario through the Ontario Media Development Corporation's Ontario Book Initiative. We further acknowledge the support of the Canada Council for the Arts and the Ontario Arts Council for our publishing program.

Acknowledgements: The Canada Council and the hospitality at 19B

Typesetting by M&S, Toronto
Printed and bound in Canada.

McClelland & Stewart Ltd.
The Canadian Publishers
481 University Avenue
Toronto, Ontario
M5G 2E9
www.mcclelland.com/NCL

4 5 6 7 8   09 08 07 06 05

As the mist leaves no scar
On the dark green hill,
So my body leaves no scar
On you, nor ever will.

When wind and hawk encounter,
What remains to keep?
So you and I encounter
Then turn, then fall to sleep.

As many nights endure
Without a moon or star,
So will we endure
When one is gone and far.

Book I

BREAVMAN KNOWS a girl named Shell whose ears were pierced so she could wear the long filigree earrings. The punctures festered and now she has a tiny scar in each earlobe. He discovered them behind her hair.

A bullet broke into the flesh of his father's arm as he rose out of a trench. It comforts a man with coronary thrombosis to bear a wound taken in combat.

On the right temple Breavman has a scar which Krantz bestowed with a shovel. Trouble over a snowman. Krantz wanted to use clinkers as eyes. Breavman was and still is against the use of foreign materials in the decoration of snowmen. No woollen mufflers, hats, spectacles. In the same vein he does not approve of inserting carrots in the mouths of carved pumpkins or pinning on cucumber ears.

His mother regarded her whole body as a scar grown over some earlier perfection which she sought in mirrors and windows and hub-caps.

Children show scars like medals. Lovers use them as secrets to reveal. A scar is what happens when the word is made flesh.

It is easy to display a wound, the proud scars of combat. It is hard to show a pimple.

2

Breavman's young mother hunted wrinkles with two hands and a magnifying mirror.

When she found one she consulted a fortress of oils and creams arrayed on a glass tray and she sighed. Without faith the wrinkle was anointed.

"This isn't my face, not my real face."

"Where is your real face, Mother?"

"Look at me. Is this what I look like?"

"Where is it, where's your real face?"

"I don't know, in Russia, when I was a girl."

He pulled the huge atlas out of the shelf and fell with it. He sifted pages like a goldminer until he found it, the whole of Russia, pale and vast. He kneeled over the distances until his eyes blurred and he made the lakes and rivers and names become an incredible face, dim and beautiful and easily lost.

The maid had to drag him to supper. A lady's face floated over the silver and the food.

3

His father lived mostly in bed or a tent in the hospital. When he was up and walking he lied.

He took his cane without the silver band and led his son over Mount Royal. Here was the ancient crater. Two iron and stone cannon rested in the gentle grassy scoop which was once a pit of boiling lava. Breavman wanted to dwell on the violence.

"We'll come back here when I'm better."

One lie.

Breavman learned to pat the noses of horses tethered

beside the Chalet, how to offer them sugar cubes from a flat palm.

"One day we'll go riding."

"But you can hardly breathe."

His father collapsed that evening over his map of flags on which he plotted the war, fumbling for the capsules to break and inhale.

4

Here is a movie filled with the bodies of his family.

His father aims the camera at his uncles, tall and serious, boutonnières in their dark lapels, who walk too close and enter into blurdom.

Their wives look formal and sad. His mother steps back, urging aunts to get into the picture. At the back of the screen her smile and shoulders go limp. She thinks she is out of focus.

Breavman stops the film to study her and her face is eaten by a spreading orange-rimmed stain as the film melts.

His grandmother sits in the shadows of the stone balcony and aunts present her with babies. A silver tea-set glows richly in early Technicolor.

His grandfather reviews a line of children but is stopped in the midst of an approving nod and ravaged by a technical orange flame.

Breavman is mutilating the film in his efforts at history.

Breavman and his cousins fight small gentlemanly battles. The girls curtsy. All the children are invited to leap one at a time across the flagstone path.

A gardener is led shy and grateful into the sunlight to be preserved with his betters.

A battalion of wives is squeezed abreast, is decimated by the edge of the screen. His mother is one of the first to go.

Suddenly the picture is shoes and blurred grass as his father staggers under another attack.

"Help!"

Coils of celluloid are burning around his feet. He dances until he is saved by Nursie and the maid and punished by his mother.

The movie runs night and day. Be careful, blood, be careful.

5

The Breavmans founded and presided over most of the institutions which make the Montreal Jewish community one of the most powerful in the world today.

The joke around the city is: The Jews are the conscience of the world and the Breavmans are the conscience of the Jews. "And I am the conscience of the Breavmans," adds Lawrence Breavman. "Actually we are the only Jews left; that is, super-Christians, first citizens with cut prongs."

The feeling today, if anyone troubles himself to articulate it, is that the Breavmans are in a decline. "Be careful," Lawrence Breavman warns his executive cousins, "or your children will speak with accents."

Ten years ago Breavman compiled the Code of Breavman:

We are Victorian gentlemen of Hebraic persuasion.

We cannot be positive, but we are fairly certain that any other Jews with money got it on the black market.

We do not wish to join Christian clubs or weaken our blood through inter-marriage. We wish to be regarded as peers, united by class, education, power, differentiated by home rituals.

We refuse to pass the circumcision line.

We were civilized first and drink less, you lousy bunch of bloodthirsty drunks.

6

A rat is more alive than a turtle.

A turtle is slow, cold, mechanical, nearly a toy, a shell with legs. Their deaths didn't count. But a white rat is quick and warm in its envelope of skin.

Krantz kept his in an empty radio. Breavman kept his in a deep honey tin. Krantz went away for the holidays and asked Breavman to take care of his. Breavman dropped it in with his.

Feeding rats is work. You have to go down to the basement. He forgot for a while. Soon he didn't want to think about the honey tin and avoided the basement stairs.

He went down at last and there was an awful smell coming from the tin. He wished it were still full of honey. He looked inside and one rat had eaten most of the stomach of the other rat. He didn't care which was his. The alive rat jumped at him and then he knew it was crazy.

He held the tin way in front because of the stink and filled it with water. The dead one floated on top with the hole between its ribs and hind legs showing. The alive one scratched the side.

He was called for lunch which began with marrow. His father tapped it out of a bone. It came from inside an animal.

When he went down again both were floating. He emptied the can in the driveway and covered it with snow. He vomited and covered that with snow.

Krantz was mad. He wanted to have a funeral at least, but they couldn't find the bodies because of some heavy snowfalls.

When Spring began they attacked islands of dirty snow in the driveway. Nothing. Krantz said that seeing things were as they were Breavman owed him money for a white rat. He'd lent his and got nothing back, not even a skeleton. Breavman said that a hospital doesn't pay anything when someone dies there. Krantz said that when you lend somebody something and that person loses it he has to pay for it. Breavman said that when it's alive it isn't a thing and besides he was doing him a favour when he took care of his. Krantz said that killing a rat was some favour and they fought it out on the wet gravel. Then they went downtown and bought new ones.

Breavman's escaped and lived in a closet under the stairs. He saw its eyes with a flashlight. For a few mornings he put out Puffed Wheat in front of the door and it was nibbled, but soon he didn't bother.

When summer came and the shutters and screens were being taken out one of the men discovered a little skeleton. It had patches of hair stuck to it. He dropped it in a garbage can.

Breavman fished it out when the man was gone and ran to Krantz's. He said it was the skeleton of the first rat and Krantz could have a funeral if he wanted. Krantz said he didn't need a stinky old skeleton, he had a live one. Breavman said that was fine but he had to admit they were quits. Krantz admitted.

Breavman buried it under the pansies, one of which his father took each morning for his buttonhole. Breavman took new interest in smelling them.

7

Come back, stern Bertha, come back and lure me up the torture tree. Remove me from the bedrooms of easy women. Extract the full due. The girl I had last night betrays the man who pays her rent.

That is how Breavman invoked the spirit of Bertha many mornings of his twenties.

Then his bones return to chicken-width. His nose retreats from impressive Semitic prominence to a childhood Gentile obscurity. Body hair blows away with the years like an ill-fated oasis. He is light enough for handbars and apple branches. The Japs and Germans are wrong.

"Play it now, Bertha?"

He has followed her to precarious parts of the tree.

"Higher!" she demands.

Even the apples are trembling. The sun catches her flute, turns the polished wood to a moment of chrome.

"Now?"

"First you have to say something about God."

"God is a jerk."

"Oh, that's nothing. I won't play for that."

The sky is blue and the clouds are moving. There is rotting fruit on the ground some miles below.

"Fug God."

"Something terribly, horribly dirty, scaredy-cat. The real word."

"Fuck God!"

He waits for the fiery wind to lift him out of his perch and leave him dismembered on the grass.

"Fuck GOD!"

Breavman sights Krantz who is lying beside a coiled hose and unravelling a baseball.

"Hey, Krantz, listen to this. *FUCK GOD!*"

Breavman never heard his own voice so pure. The air is a microphone.

Bertha alters her fragile position to strike his cheek with her flute.

"Dirty tongue!"

"It was your idea."

She strikes again for piety and tears off apples as she crashes past the limbs. Nothing of her voice as she falls.

Krantz and Breavman survey her for one second twisted into a position she could never achieve in gym. Her bland Saxon face is further anesthetized by uncracked steel-rimmed glasses. A sharp bone of the arm has escaped the skin.

After the ambulance Breavman whispered.

"Krantz, there's something special about my voice."

"No, there isn't."

"There is so. I can make things happen."

"You're a nut."

"Want to hear my resolutions?"

"No."

"I promise not to speak for a week. I promise to learn how to play it myself. In that way the number of people who know how to play remains the same."

"What good's that?"

"It's obvious, Krantz."

8

His father decided to rise from his chair.

"I'm speaking to you, Lawrence!"

"Your father's speaking to you, Lawrence," his mother interpreted.

Breavman attempted one last desperate pantomime.

"Listen to your father breathing."

The elder Breavman calculated the expense of energy, accepted the risk, drove the back of his hand across his son's face.

His lips were not too swollen to practise 'Old Black Joe'.

They said she'd live. But he didn't give it up. He'd be one extra.

9

The Japs and Germans were beautiful enemies. They had buck teeth or cruel monocles and commanded in crude English with much saliva. They started the war because of their nature.

Red Cross ships must be bombed, all parachutists

machine-gunned. Their uniforms were stiff and decorated with skulls. They kept right on eating and laughed at appeals for mercy.

They did nothing warlike without a close-up of perverted glee.

Best of all, they tortured. To get secrets, to make soap, to set examples to towns of heroes. But mostly they tortured for fun, because of their nature.

Comic books, movies, radio programmes centred their entertainment around the fact of torture. Nothing fascinates a child like a tale of torture. With the clearest of consciences, with a patriotic intensity, children dreamed, talked, acted orgies of physical abuse. Imaginations were released to wander on a reconnaissance mission from Calvary to Dachau.

European children starved and watched their parents scheme and die. Here we grew up with toy whips. Early warning against our future leaders, the war babies.

10

They had Lisa, they had the garage, they needed string, red string for the sake of blood.

They couldn't enter the deep garage without red string.

Breavman remembered a coil.

The kitchen drawer is a step removed from the garbage can which is a step removed from the outside garbage can, which is a step removed from the armadillo-hulked automatic garbage trucks, which are a step removed from the mysterious stinking garbage heaps by the edge of the St. Lawrence.

"A nice glass of chocolate milk?"

He wished his mother had some respect for importance.

Oh, it is a most perfect kitchen drawer, even when you are in a desperate hurry.

Besides the tangled string box there are candle-butts from

years of Sabbath evenings kept in thrifty anticipation of hurricanes, brass keys to locks which have been changed (it is difficult to throw out anything so precise and crafted as a metal key), straight pens with ink-caked nibs which could be cleaned if anyone took the trouble (his mother instructed the maid), toothpicks they never used (especially for picking teeth), the broken pair of scissors (the new pair was kept in another drawer: ten years later it was still referred to as 'the new pair'), exhausted rubber rings from home preserving bottles (pickled tomatoes, green, evil, tight-skinned), knobs, nuts, all the homey debris which avarice protects.

He fingered blindly in the string box because the drawer can never be opened all the way.

"A little cooky, a nice piece of honey cake, there's a whole box of macaroons?"

Ah! bright red.

The welts dance all over Lisa's imaginary body.

"Strawberries," his mother called like a good-bye.

There is a way children enter garages, barns, attics, the same way they enter great halls and family chapels. Garages, barns and attics are always older than the buildings to which they are attached. They have the dark reverent air of immense kitchen drawers. They are friendly museums.

It was dark inside, smelled of oil and last year's leaves which splintered as they moved. Bits of metal, the edges of shovels and cans glimmered damply.

"You're the American," said Krantz.

"No, I'm not," said Lisa.

"You're the American," said Breavman. "Two against one."

The ack-ack of Breavman and Krantz was very heavy. Lisa came on a daring manoeuvre across the darkness, arms outstretched.

"Eheheheheheheh," stuttered her machine guns.

She's hit.

She went into a spectacular nose dive, bailed out at the last moment. Swaying from one foot to another she floated down the sky, looking below, knowing her number was up.

She's a perfect dancer, Breavman thought.

Lisa watched the Krauts coming.

"*Achtung. Heil Hitler!* You are a prisoner of the Third Reich."

"I swallowed the plans."

"Vee haf methods."

She is led to lie face down on the cot.

"Just on the bum."

Geez, they're white, they're solid white.

Her buttocks were whipped painlessly with red string.

"Turn over," Breavman commanded.

"The rule was: only on the bum," Lisa protested.

"That was last time," argued Krantz the legalist.

She had to take off her top, too, and the cot disappeared from under her and she floated in the autumnal gloom of the garage, two feet above the stone floor.

Oh my, my, my.

Breavman didn't take his turn whipping. There were white flowers growing out of all her pores.

"What's the matter with him? I'm getting dressed."

"The Third Reich vill not tolerate insubordination," said Krantz.

"Should we hold her?" said Breavman.

"She'll make a lot of noise," said Krantz.

Now outside of the game, she made them turn while she put on her dress. The sunlight she let in while leaving turned the garage into a garage. They sat in silence, the red whip lost.

"Let's go, Breavman."

"She's perfect, isn't she, Krantz?"

"What's so perfect about her?"

"You saw her. She's perfect."

"So long, Breavman."

Breavman followed him out of the yard.

"She's perfect, Krantz, didn't you see?"

Krantz plugged his ears with his forefingers. They passed Bertha's Tree. Krantz began to run.

"She was really perfect, you have to admit it, Krantz."

Krantz was faster.

11

One of Breavman's early sins was to sneak a look at the gun. His father kept it in a night-table between his and his wife's bed.

It was a huge .38 in a thick leather case. Name, rank and regiment engraved on the barrel. Lethal, angular, precise, it smouldered in the dark drawer with dangerous potential. The metal was always cold.

The sound of the machinery when Breavman pulled the hammer back was the marvellous sound of all murderous scientific achievement. Click! like the smacking of cogwheel lips.

The little blunt bullets took the scratch of a thumbnail.

If there were Germans coming down the street . . .

When his father married he swore to kill any man who ever made advances towards his wife. His mother told the story as a joke. Breavman believed the words. He had a vision of a corpse-heap of all the men who had ever smiled at her.

His father had an expensive heart doctor named Farley. He was around so much that they might have called him Uncle if they had been that sort of family. While his father was gasping under the oxygen-tent in the Royal Victoria, Doctor Farley kissed his mother in the hallway of their house. It was a gentle kiss to console an unhappy woman, between two people who had known each other through many crises.

Breavman wondered whether or not he'd better get the gun and finish him off.

Then who'd repair his father?

Not long ago Breavman watched his mother read the *Star*. She put down the paper and a Chekhovian smile of lost orchards softened her face. She had just read Farley's obituary notice.

"Such a handsome man." She seemed to be thinking of sad Joan Crawford movies. "He wanted me to marry him."

"Before or after my father died?"

"Don't be so foolish."

His father was a tidy man, upturned his wife's sewing basket when he thought it was getting messy, raged when his family's slippers were not carefully lined under respective beds.

He was a fat man who laughed easily with everybody but his brothers.

He was so fat and his brothers were tall and thin and it wasn't fair, it wasn't fair, why should the fat one die, didn't he have enough being fat and breathless, why not one of the handsome ones?

The gun proved he was once a warrior.

His brother's pictures were in the papers in connection with the war effort. He gave his son his first book, *The Romance of the King's Army*, a thick volume praising British regiments.

K-K-K-Katy, he sang when he could.

What he really loved was machinery. He would go miles to see a machine which cut a pipe this way instead of that. His family thought him a fool. He lent money to his friends and employees without question. He was given poetry books for his bar-mitzvah. Breavman has the leather books now and startles at each uncut page.

"And read these, too, Lawrence."

> *How To Tell Birds*
> *How To Tell Trees*
> *How To Tell Insects*
> *How To Tell Stones*

He looked at his father in the crisp, white bed, always neat, still smelling of Vitalis. There was something sour inside the softening body, some enemy, some limpness of the heart.

He tore the books as his father weakened. He didn't know why he hated the careful diagrams and coloured plates. We do. It was to scorn the world of detail, information, precision, all the false knowledge which cannot intrude on decay.

Breavman roamed his house waiting for a shot to ring out. That would teach them, the great successes, the eloquent speakers, the synagogue builders, all the grand brothers that walked ahead into public glory. He waited for the blast of a .3 which would clean the house and bring a terrible change. The gun was right beside the bed. He waited for his father to execute his heart.

"Get me the medals out of the top drawer."

Breavman brought them to the bed. The reds and golds of the ribbons ran into each other as in a watercolour. With some effort his father pinned them on Breavman's sweater.

Breavman stood at attention ready to receive the farewell address.

"Don't you like them? You're always looking at them."

"Oh, yes."

"Stop stretching yourself like a damn fool. They're yours."

"Thank you, sir."

"Well, go out and play with them. Tell your mother I don't want to see anyone and that includes my famous brothers."

Breavman went downstairs and unlocked the closet which held his father's fishing equipment. He spent hours in wonder putting the great salmon rods together, winding and unwinding the copper wire, handling the dangerous flies and hooks.

How could his father have wielded these beautiful, heavy weapons, that swollen body on the crisp, white bed?

Where was the body in rubber boots that waded up rivers,

12

Many years later, telling all this, Breavman interrupted himself:

"Shell, how many men know of those little scars in your earlobes? How many besides me, the original archaeologist of earlobes?"

"Not as many as you think."

"I don't mean the two or three or fifty that kissed them with their everyday lips. But in your fantasies, how many did something impossible with their mouths?"

"Lawrence, please, we're lying here together. You're trying to spoil the night somehow."

"I'd say battalions."

She did not reply and her silence removed her body from him a little distance.

"Tell me some more about Bertha, Krantz and Lisa."

"Anything I tell you is an alibi for something else."

"Then let's be quiet together."

"I saw Lisa before that time in the garage. We must have been five or six."

Breavman stared at Shell and described Lisa's sunny room, dense with expensive toys. Electric hobby-horse which rocked itself. Life-sized walking dolls. Nothing that didn't squeak or light up when squeezed.

They hid in the shade of under-the-bed, their hands full of secrets and new smells, on the look-out for servants, watching the sun slide along the linoleum with the fairy tales cut in it.

The gigantic shoes of a housemaid paddled close by.

"That's lovely, Lawrence."

"But it's a lie. It happened, but it's a lie. Bertha's Tree is a lie although she really fell out of it. That night after I fooled with

my father's fishing rods I sneaked into my parents' room. The
were both sleeping in their separate beds. There was a moor
They were both facing the ceiling and lying in the same posi
tion. I knew that if I shouted only one of them would wake
up."

"Was that the night he died?"

"It doesn't matter how anything happens."

He began to kiss her shoulders and face and although h
was hurting her with his nails and teeth she didn't protest

"Your body will never be familiar."

13

After breakfast six men entered the house and set the coffi
down in the living-room. It was surprisingly huge, made o
dark-grained wood, brass-handled. There was snow on thei
clothes.

The room was suddenly more formal than Breavman ha
ever known it. His mother squinted.

They placed it on a stand and began to open the cabinet
like cover.

"Close it, close it, we're not in Russia!"

Breavman shut his eyes and waited for the click of th
cover. But these men who make their living among th
bereaved move noiselessly. They were gone when he opene
his eyes.

"Why did you make them close it, Mother?"

"It's enough as it is."

The mirrors of the house were soaped, as if the glass ha
become victim to a strange indoor frost corresponding to th
wide winter. His mother stayed alone in her room. Breavma
sat stiffly on his bed and tried to fight his anger with a softe
emotion.

The coffin was parallel to the chesterfield.

Whispering people began to congregate in the hall and on the balcony.

Breavman and his mother descended the stairs. The afternoon winter sun glimmered on his mother's black stockings and gave to the mourners in the doorway a gold outline. He could see parked cars and dirty snow above their heads.

They stood closest, his uncles behind them. Friends and workers from the family factory thronged the hall, balcony, and path. His uncles, tall and solemn, touched his shoulders with their manicured hands.

But his mother was defeated. The coffin was open.

He was swaddled in silk, wrapped in a silvered prayer-shawl. His moustache bloomed fierce and black against his white face. He appeared annoyed, as if he were about to awaken, climb out of the offensively ornate box, and resume his sleep on the more comfortable chesterfield.

The cemetery was like an Alpine town, the stones like little sleeping houses. The diggers looked irreverently informal in their working clothes. A mat of artificial grass was spread over the heaps of exhumed frozen mud. The coffin went down in a system of pulleys.

Bagels and hard-boiled eggs, shapes of eternity, were served back at the house. His uncles joked with friends of the family. Breavman hated them. He looked under his great-uncle's beard and asked him why he didn't wear a tie.

He was the oldest son of the oldest son.

The family left last. Funerals are so neat. All they left behind were small gold-rimmed plates flecked with crumbs and caraway seeds.

The yards of lace curtain held some of the light of the small winter moon.

"Did you look at him, Mother?"

"Of course."

"He looked mad, didn't he?"

"Poor boy."

"And his moustache really black. As if it was done with an eyebrow pencil."

"It's late, Lawrence . . ."

"It's late, all right. We'll never see him again."

"I forbid you to use that voice to your mother."

"Why did you make them close it? Why did you? We could have seen him for a whole extra morning."

"Go to bed!"

"Christ you, christ you, bastardess, witch!" he improvised in a scream.

All night he heard his mother in the kitchen, weeping and eating.

14

Here is a colour photograph, largest picture on a wall of ancestors.

His father wears an English suit and all the English reticence that can be woven into cloth. A wine tie with a tiny, hard knot sprouts like a gargoyle. In his lapel a Canadian Legion pin, duller than jewellery. The double-chinned face glows with Victorian reason and decency, though the hazel eyes are a little too soft and staring, the mouth too full, Semitic, hurt.

The fierce moustache presides over the sensitive lips like a suspicious trustee.

The blood, which he died spitting, is invisible, but forms on the chin as Breavman studies the portrait.

He is one of the princes of Breavman's private religion, double-natured and arbitrary. He is the persecuted brother, the near poet, the innocent of the machine toys, the sighing judge who listens but does not sentence.

Also he is heaving Authority, armoured with Divine Right, doing merciless violence to all that is weak, taboo, un-Breavmanlike.

As Breavman does him homage he wonders whether his father is just listening or whether he is stamping the seal on decrees.

Now he is settling more passively into his gold frame and his expression has become as distant as those in the older photographs. His clothes begin to appear dated and costume-like. He can rest. Breavman has inherited all his concerns.

The day after the funeral Breavman split open one of his father's formal bow ties and sewed in a message. He buried it in the garden, under the snow beside the fence where in summer the neighbour's lilies-of-the-valley infiltrate.

15

Lisa had straight black Cleopatra hair that bounced in sheaves off her shoulders when she ran or jumped. Her legs were long and well-formed, made beautiful by natural exercise. Her eyes were big, heavy-lidded, dreamy.

Breavman thought that perhaps she dreamed as he did, of intrigue and high deeds, but no, her wide eyes were roaming in imagination over the well-appointed house she was to govern, the brood she was to mother, the man she was to warm.

They grew tired of games in the field beside Bertha's Tree. They did not want to squeeze under someone's porch for Sardines. They did not want to limp through Hospital Tag. They did not want to draw the magic circle and sign it with a dot. Ildish-chay. Ets-lay o-gay, they whispered. They didn't care who was It.

Better games of flesh, love, curiosity. They walked away from Run-Sheep-Run over to the park and sat on a bench near the pond where nurses gossip and children aim their toy boats.

He wanted to know everything about her. Was she allowed to listen to The Shadow ("The weed of crime bears bitter fruit.

Who knows what evil lurks in the hearts of men? The Shadow knows, hehehehehehheheh")? Wasn't Alan Young terrific? Especially the character with the flighty voice, "I'm hyah, I'm hyah, come gather rosebuds from my hair." Wasn't the only decent part of the Charlie McCarthy programme when Mortimer Snerd came on? Could she get *Gangbusters*? Did she want to hear him imitate the Green Hornet's car, driven by his faithful Filipino valet, Cato, or the Whistler? Wasn't that a beautiful tune?

Had she ever been called a Dirty Jew?

They fell silent and the nurses and their blond babies reasserted their control of the universe.

And what was it like to have no father?

It made you more grown-up. You carved the chicken, you sat where he sat.

Lisa listened, and Breavman, for the first time, felt himself dignified, or rather, dramatized. His father's death gave him a touch of mystery, contact with the unknown. He could speak with extra authority on God and Hell.

The nurses gathered their children and their boats and went away. The surface of the pond became smooth. The hands of the clock on the Chalet wound towards supper-time, but they kept on talking.

They squeezed hands, kissed once when the light was low enough, coming golden through the prickly bushes. Then they walked slowly home, not holding hands, but bumping against each other.

Breavman sat at the table trying to understand why he wasn't hungry. His mother extolled the lamb chops.

16

Whenever they could they played their great game, The Soldier and the Whore. They played it in whatever room they could. He was on leave from the front and she was a whore of DeBullion Street.

Knock, knock, the door opened slowly.

They shook hands and he tickled her palm with his forefinger.

Thus they participated in that mysterious activity the accuracies of which the adults keep so coyly hidden with French words, with Yiddish words, with spelled-out words; that veiled ritual about which night-club comedians construct their humour; that unapproachable knowledge which grownups guard to guarantee their authority.

Their game forbade talking dirty or roughhouse. They had no knowledge of the sordid aspect of brothels, and who knows if there is one? They thought of them as some sort of pleasure palace, places denied them as arbitrarily as Montreal movie theatres.

Whores were ideal women just as soldiers were ideal men.

"Pay me now?"

"Here's all my money, beautiful baby."

17

Seven to eleven is a huge chunk of life, full of dulling and forgetting. It is fabled that we slowly lose the gift of speech with animals, that birds no longer visit our windowsills to converse. As our eyes grow accustomed to sight they armour themselves against wonder. Flowers once the size of pine trees return to clay pots. Even terror diminishes. The giants and giantesses of the nursery shrink to crabby teachers and human fathers. Breavman forgot everything he learned from Lisa's small body.

Oh, how their lives had emptied from the time they crawled out from under the bed and stood up on their hind legs!

Now they longed for knowledge but undressing was a sin. Therefore they were an easy touch for the postcards, pornographic magazines, home-made erotica peddled in school cloakrooms. They became connoisseurs of sculpture and painting. They knew all the books in the library which had the best, most revealing reproductions.

What did bodies look like?

Lisa's mother presented her with a careful book and they searched it in vain for straight information. There were phrases like "the temple of the human body," which may be true, but where was it, with its hair and creases? They wanted clear pictures, not a blank page with a dot in the centre and a breathless caption: 'Just think! the male sperm is 1,000 times smaller than this.'

So they wore light clothing. He had a pair of green shorts which she loved for their thinness. She had a yellow dress which he preferred. This situation gave birth to Lisa's great lyric exclamation:

"You wear your green silk pants tomorrow; I'll wear my yellow dress, so it'll be better."

Deprivation is the mother of poetry.

He was about to send for a volume advertised in a confession magazine which promised to arrive in a plain, brown wrapper, when, in one of the periodic searches through the maid's drawers, he found the viewer.

It was made in France and contained a two-foot strip of film. You held it to the light and turned the little round knob and you saw everything.

Let us praise this film, which has disappeared with the maid into the Canadian wilderness.

It was titled in English, with beguiling simplicity, "Thirty Ways to Screw". The scenes were nothing like the pornographic movies Breavman later witnessed and attacked, of naked, jumpy men and women acting out the contrived, sordid plots.

The actors were handsome humans, happy in their film career. They were not the scrawny, guilty, desperately gay cast-offs who perform for gentlemen's smokers. There were no lecherous smiles for the camera, no winking and lip-licking, no abuse of the female organ with cigarettes and beer bottles, no ingenious unnatural arrangement of bodies.

Each frame glowed with tenderness and passionate delight.

This tiny strip of celluloid shown widely in Canadian theatres might revitalize the tedious marriages which are reported to abound in our country.

Where are you, working girl with supreme device? The National Film Board hath need of you. Are you growing old in Winnipeg?

The film ended with a demonstration of the grand, democratic, universal practice of physical love. There were Indian couples represented, Chinese, Negro, Arabian, all without their national costumes on.

Come back, maid, strike a blow for World Federalism.

They pointed the viewer to the window and solemnly traded it back and forth.

They knew it would be like this.

The window gave over the slope of Murray Park, across the commercial city, down to the Saint Lawrence, American mountains in the distance. When it wasn't his turn Breavman took in the prospect. Why was anybody working?

They were two children hugging in a window, breathless with wisdom.

They could not rush to it then and there. They weren't safe from intrusion. Not only that, children have a highly developed sense of ritual and formality. This was important. They had to decide whether they were in love. Because if there was one thing the pictures showed, you had to be in love. They thought they were but they would give themselves a week just to make sure.

They hugged again in what they thought would be among their last fully clothed embraces.

How can Breavman have regrets? It was Nature herself who intervened.

Three days before Thursday, maid's day off, they met in their special place, the bench beside the pond in the park. Lisa was shy but determined to be straight and honest, as was her nature.

"I can't do it with you."

"Aren't your parents going away?"

"It's not that. Last night I got the Curse."

She touched his hand with pride.

"Oh."

"Know what I mean?"

"Sure."

He hadn't the remotest idea.

"But it would still be O.K., wouldn't it?"

"But now I can have babies. Mummy told me about everything last night. She had it all ready for me, too, napkins, a belt of my own, everything."

"No guff?"

What was she talking about? The Curse sounded like a celestial intrusion on his pleasure.

"She told me about all the stuff, just like the camera."

"Did you tell her about the camera?"

Nothing, the world, nobody could be trusted.

"She promised not to tell anyone."

"It was a secret."

"Don't be sad. We had a long talk. I told her about us, too. You see, I've got to act like a lady now. Girls have to act older than boys."

"Who's sad?"

She leaned back in the bench and took his hand.

"But aren't you happy for me?" she laughed, "that I got the Curse? I have it right now!"

18

Soon she was deep in the rites of young womanhood. She came back from camp half a head taller than Breavman, with breasts that disturbed even bulky sweaters.

"Hiya, Lisa."

"Hello, Lawrence."

She was meeting her mother downtown, she was flying to New York for clothes. She was dressed with that kind of austerity which can make any thirteen-year-old a poignant beauty. None of the uglyfying extravagance to which Westmount Jews and Gentiles are currently devoted.

Good-bye.

He watched her grow away from him, not with sadness but with wonder. At fifteen she was a grand lady who wore traces of lipstick and was allowed an occasional cigarette.

He sat in their old window and saw the older boys call for her in their fathers' cars. He marvelled that he had ever kissed the mouth that now mastered cigarettes. Seeing her ushered into these long cars by young men with white scarves, seeing her sitting like a duchess in a carriage while they closed the door and walked briskly in front of the machine and climbed importantly into the driver's seat, he had to convince himself that he had ever had a part in that beauty and grace.

Hey, you forgot one of your little fragrances on my thumb.

19

Fur gloves in the sun-room.

Certain years the sun-room, which was no more than an enclosed balcony attached to the back of the house, was used to store some of the winter clothes.

Breavman, Krantz and Philip came into this room for no particular reason. They looked out of the windows at the park and the tennis players.

There was the regular sound of balls hit back and forth and the hysterical sound of a house fly battering a window pane.

Breavman's father was dead, Krantz's was away most of the time, but Philip's was strict. He did not let Philip wear his hair with a big pompadour in front. He had to slick it down to his scalp with some nineteenth-century hair tonic.

That historic afternoon Philip looked around and what did he spy but a pair of fur gloves.

He pulled on one of them, sat himself down on a pile of blankets.

Breavman and Krantz, who were perceptive children, understood that the fur glove was not an integral part of the practice.

They all agreed it smelt like Javel water. Philip washed it down the sink.

"Catholics think it's a sin," he instructed.

20

Breavman and Shell were beside the lake. The evening mist was piling up along the opposite shore like dunes of sand. They lay in a double sleeping bag beside the fire, which was built of driftwood they had gathered that afternoon. He wanted to tell her everything.

"I still do."

"Me too," she said.

"I read that Rousseau did right to the end of his life. I guess a certain kind of creative person is like that. He works all day to discipline his imagination so it's there he's most at home. No real corporeal woman can give him the pleasure of his own creations. Shell, don't let me scare you with what I'm saying."

"But doesn't it separate us completely?"

They held hands tightly and watched the stars in the dark part of the sky; where the moon was bright they were obliterated. She told him she loved him.

A loon went insane in the middle of the lake.

21

After that distinguished summer of yellow dresses and green pants Lisa and Breavman rarely met. But once, during the following winter, they wrestled in the snow.

That episode has a circumference for Breavman, a kind of black-edged picture frame separating it from what he remembers of her.

It was after Hebrew school. They found themselves starting home together. They cut up through the park. There was almost a full moon and it silvered the snow.

The light seemed to come from under the snow. When they broke the crust with their boots the powdered snow beneath was brighter.

They tried to walk on the crust without breaking it. Both carried their Hebrew books, particular sections of the Torah which they were studying at the time.

Competition in crust-walking led to other trials: snowballing, tests of balance on the icy parts, pushing, and finally personal combat which began jovially but ended in serious struggle.

This was on the slope of the hill, near a line of poplar trees. Breavman recalls it as like a Brueghel: two small bulky-coated figures entwined, their limited battle viewed through icy branches.

At a certain point Breavman discovered he wasn't going to win. He strained to topple her, he could not. He felt himself slipping. They were still holding their Hebrew books. He dropped his in a last-ditch effort at an offensive but it failed and he went down.

The snow was not cold. Lisa stood above him in strange female triumph. He ate some snow.

"And you have to kiss the Sidur."

It was mandatory to kiss a holy book which had fallen to the ground.

"Like hell I do!"

He crawled to his books, gathered them contemptuously and stood up.

What Breavman remembers most clearly of that struggle is the cold moonlight and the crisp trees, and the humiliation of a defeat which was not only bitter but unnatural.

22

He read everything he could on hypnosis. He hid the books behind a curtain and studied by flashlight.

Here was the real world.

There was a long section, "How to Hypnotize Animals." Terrifying illustration of glassy-eyed roosters.

Breavman pictured himself a militant Saint Francis, commanding the world by means of his loyal herds and flocks. Apes as obedient satraps. Clouds of pigeons ready to commit suicide against enemy planes. Hyena bodyguards. Massed triumphal choruses of nightingales.

Tovarich, named before the Stalin-Hitler pact, slept on the porch in the afternoon sun. Breavman squatted and swung the pendulum he had made out of a drilled silver dollar. The dog opened its eyes, sniffed to assure itself it was not food, returned to sleep.

But was it natural sleep?

The neighbours had a cartoon of a Dachshund named Cognac. Breavman looked for a slave in the gold eyes.

It worked!

Or was it just the lazy, humid afternoon?

He had to climb a fence to get at Lisa's Fox Terrier which he fixed in a sitting position inches from a bowl of Pard.

You will be highly favoured, dog of Lisa.

After his fifth success the exhilaration of his dark power carried him along the boulevard, running blindly and laughing.

A whole street of dogs frozen! The city lay before him. He would have an agent in every house. All he had to do was whistle.

Maybe Krantz deserved a province.

Whistle, that's all. But there was no point in threatening a vision with such a crude test. He shoved his hands down his pockets and floated home on the secret of his revolution.

23

In those dark ages, early adolescence, he was almost a head shorter than most of his friends.

But it was his friends who were humiliated when he had to stand on a stool to see over the pulpit when he sang his bar mitzvah. It didn't matter to him how he faced the congregation: his great-grandfather had built the synagogue.

Short boys were supposed to take out shorter girls. That was the rule. He knew the tall uneasy girls he wanted could easily be calmed by stories and talk.

His friends insisted that his size was a terrible affliction and they convinced him. They convinced him with inches of flesh and bone.

He didn't know their mystery of how bodies were increased, how air and food worked for them. How did they cajole the universe? Why was the sky holding out on him?

He began to think of himself as The Tiny Conspirator, The Cunning Dwarf.

He worked frantically on a pair of shoes. He had ripped off the heels of an old pair and tried to hammer them on to his own. The rubber didn't hold the nails very well. He'd have to be careful.

This was in the deep basement of his house, traditional workshop of bomb-throwers and confusers of society.

There he stood, an inch taller, feeling a mixture of shame and craftiness. Nothing like brains, eh? He waltzed round the concrete floor and fell on his face.

He had completely forgotten the desperation of a few minutes before. It came back to him as he sat painfully on the floor, looking up at a naked bulb. The detached heel which had tripped him crouched like a rodent a couple of feet away, nails protruding like sharpened fangs.

The party was fifteen minutes away. And Muffin went around with an older, therefore taller group.

Rumour had it that Muffin stuffed her bra with Kleenex. He decided to apply the technique. Carefully he laid a Kleenex platform into each shoe. It raised his heels almost to the rims of the leather. He let his trousers ride low.

A few spins around the concrete and he satisfied himself that he could manoeuvre. Panic eased. Science triumphed again.

Fluorescent lights hid in a false moulding lit the ceiling. There was the usual mirrored bar with miniature bottles and glass knick-knacks. An upholstered seat lined one wall, on which was painted a pastel mural of drinkers of different nationalities. The Breavmans did not approve of finished basements.

He danced well for one half hour and then his feet began to ache. The Kleenex had become misshapen under his arches. After two more jitterbug records he could hardly walk. He went into the bathroom and tried to straighten the Kleenex but it was compressed into a hard ball. He thought of removing it altogether but he imagined the surprised and horrified look of the company at his shrunken stature.

He slipped his foot half-way into the shoe, placed the ball between his heel and the inside sole, stepped in hard, and tied the lace. The pain spiked up through his ankles.

The Bunny Hop nearly put him away. In the middle of that line, squashed between the girl whose waist he was holding and the girl who was holding his waist, the music loud and repetitive, everyone chanting one, two, one-two-three, his feet getting out of control because of the pain, he thought: this must be what Hell is like, an eternal Bunny Hop with sore feet, which you can never drop out of.

She with her false tits, me with my false feet, oh you evil Kleenex Company!

One of the fluorescent lights was flickering. There was disease in the walls. Maybe everyone there, every single person in the bobbing line was wearing a Kleenex prop. Maybe some had Kleenex noses and Kleenex ears and Kleenex hands. Depression seized him.

Now it was his favourite song. He wanted to dance close to Muffin, close his eyes against her hair which had just been washed.

> . . . *the girl I call my own*
> *will wear cotton and laces and smell of cologne.*

But he could barely stand up. He had to keep shifting his weight from foot to foot to dole out the pain in equal shares. Often these shifts did not correspond to the rhythm of the music and imparted to his already imperfect dancing an extra jerky quality. As his hobbling became more pronounced he was obliged to hold Muffin tighter and tighter to keep his balance.

"Not here," she whispered in his ear. "My parents won't be home till late."

Not even this pleasant invitation could assuage his discomfort. He clung to her and manoeuvred into a crowded part of the floor where he could justifiably limit his movements.

"Oh, Larry!"

"Fast worker!"

Even by the sophisticated standards of this older group he was dancing adventurously close. He accepted the cavalier role his pain cast, and bit her ear, having heard that ears were bitten.

"Let's get rid of the lights," he snarled to all men of daring.

They started from the party, and the walk was a forced march of Bataan proportions. By walking very close he made his lameness into a display of affection. On the hills the Kleenex slipped back under his arches.

A fog-horn from the city's river reached Westmount, and the sound shivered him.

"I've got to tell you something, Muffin. Then you've got to tell me something."

Muffin didn't want to sit on the grass because of her dress, but maybe he was going to ask her to go steady. She'd refuse, but what a beautiful party that would make it. The confession he was about to offer shortened his breath, and he confused his fear with love.

He tugged off his shoes, scooped out the balls of Kleenex and laid them like a secret in her lap.

Muffin's nightmare had just begun.

"Now you take yours out."

"What are you talking about?" she demanded in a voice which surprised her because it sounded so much like her mother's.

Breavman pointed to her heart.

"Don't be ashamed. You take yours out."

He reached for her top button and received his balls of Kleenex in the face.

"Get away!"

Breavman decided to let her run. Her house wasn't that far away. He wiggled his toes and rubbed his soles. He wasn't condemned to a Bunny Hop after all, not with those people. He pitched the Kleenex into the gutter and trotted home, shoes in hand.

He detoured to the park and raced over the damp ground until the view stopped him. He set down his shoes like neat lieutenants beside his feet.

He looked in awe at the expanse of night-green foliage, the austere lights of the city, the dull gleam of the St. Lawrence.

A city was a great achievement, bridges were fine things to build. But the street, harbours, spikes of stone were ultimately lost in the wider cradle of mountain and sky.

It ran a chill through his spine to be involved in the mysterious mechanism of city and black hills.

Father, I'm ignorant.

He would master the rules and techniques of the city, why the one-way streets were chosen, how the stock-market worked, what notaries did.

It wasn't a hellish Bunny Hop if you knew the true names of things. He would study leaves and bark, and visit stone quarries as his father had done.

Good-bye, world of Kleenex.

He gathered his shoes, walked into the bushes, climbed the fence which separated his house from the park.

Black lines, like an ink drawing of a storm, plunged out of the sky to help him over, he could have sworn. The house he entered was important as a museum.

24

Krantz had a reputation for being wild, having been spotted from time to time smoking two cigarettes at once on obscure Westmount streets.

He was small and wiry, his face triangular, with almost

Oriental eyes. A portrait in the dining-room of his house, painted, as his mother is fond of informing people, by the artist who "did the Governor-General's," shows an elfish boy with pointed ears, black, curly hair, butterfly lips as in a Rossetti, and an expression of good-natured superiority, an aloofness (even at that age) which is so calm that it disturbs no one.

They sat one night on someone's lawn, two Talmudists, delighting in their dialectic, which was a disguise for love. It was furious talk, the talk of a boy discovering how good it was not to be alone.

"Krantz, I know you hate this kind of question, but if you'd care to make an off-hand statement, it would be appreciated. To your knowledge, that is, the extent of your information, is there anyone on this planet who approaches the dullness of the Canadian Prime Minister?"

"Rabbi Swort?"

"Krantz, do you honestly submit that Rabbi Swort, who, as the world knows, is not exactly the Messiah or even a minor messenger of the Redemption, do you seriously suggest that Rabbi Swort challenges the utter and complete boringness of our national leader?"

"I do, Breavman, I do."

"I suppose you have your reasons, Krantz."

"I do, Breavman, you know I do."

There were once giants on the earth.

They swore not to be fooled by long cars, screen love, the Red Menace, or *The New Yorker* magazine.

Giants in unmarked graves.

All right, it's fine that people don't starve, that epidemics are controlled, that the classics are available as comics, but what about the corny old verities, truth and fun?

The fashion model was not their idea of grace, the Bomb not their idea of power, Sabbath Service not their idea of God.

"Krantz, is it true that we are Jewish?"

"So it has been rumoured, Breavman."

"Do you feel Jewish, Krantz?"

"Thoroughly."

"Do your teeth feel Jewish?"

"Especially my teeth, to say nothing of my left ball."

"We really shouldn't joke, what we were just saying reminds me of pictures from the camps."

"True."

Weren't they supposed to be a holy people consecrated to purity, service, spiritual honesty? Weren't they a nation set apart?

Why had the idea of a jealously guarded sanctity degenerated into a sly contempt for the goy, empty of self-criticism?

Parents were traitors.

They had sold their sense of destiny for an Israeli victory in the desert. Charity had become a social competition in which nobody gave away anything he really needed, like a penny-toss, the prizes being the recognition of wealth and a high place in the Donor's Book.

Smug traitors who believed spiritual fulfilment had been achieved because Einstein and Heifetz are Jews.

If only they could find the right girls. Then they could fight their way out of the swamp. Not Kleenex girls.

Breavman wonders how many miles through Montreal streets he and Krantz have driven and walked, on the look-out for the two girls who had been chosen cosmically to be their companion-mistresses. Hot summer evenings casing the mobs in La Fontaine Park, looking searchingly into young female eyes, they knew that at any moment two beauties would detach themselves from the crowd and take their arms. Krantz at the wheel of his father's Buick, steering between hedges of snow piled on either side of the narrow back streets in the east end, at a crawling speed because there was a blizzard going on, they knew that two shivering figures would emerge from a doorway, tap timidly on the frosted windows of the car, and it would be they.

If they had the right seats on the loop-the-loop the girls' hair would blow against their faces. If they went up north for a ski weekend and stayed at the right hotel they would hear the beautiful sound of girls undressing in the room next door. And if they walked twelve miles along St. Catherine Street, there was no telling whom they'd meet.

"I can get the Lincoln tonight, Breavman."

"Great. It'll be packed downtown."

"Great. We'll drive around."

So they would drive, like American tourists on the make, almost lost in the front seat of one of the huge Krantzstone automobiles, until everyone had gone home and the streets were empty. Still they continued their prowl because the girls they wanted might prefer deserted streets. Then when it was clear that they weren't coming that particular night they'd head out to the lake shore, and circle the black water of Lac St. Louis.

"What do you think it's like to drown, Krantz?"

"You're supposed to black out after you take in a fairly small amount of water."

"How much, Krantz?"

"You're supposed to be able to drown in a bathtub."

"In a glass of water, Krantz."

"In a damp rag, Breavman."

"In a moist Kleenex. Hey, Krantz, that would be a great way to kill a guy, with water. You get the guy and use an eyedropper on him, a squirt at a time. They find him drowned in his study. Big mystery."

"Wouldn't work, Breavman. How would you hold him still? There'd be bruise marks or rope marks on him."

"But if it could work. They find the guy slumped over his desk and nobody knows how he died. Coroner's inquest: death by drowning. And he hasn't been to the sea-shore in ten years."

"Germans used a lot of water in their tortures. They'd shove a hose up a guy's arse-hole to make him talk."

"Great, Krantz. Japs had something like that. They'd make a guy eat a lot of uncooked rice then he'd have to drink a gallon of water. The rice would swell and —"

"Yeah, I heard that one."

"But, Krantz, want to hear the worst one? And it was the Americans who did it. Listen, they catch a Jap on the battle-field and make him swallow five or six rifle cartridges. Then they'd make him run and jump. The cartridges'd rip his stomach apart. He'd die of internal haemorrhage. American soldiers."

"How about tossing babies in the air for bayonet practice?"

"Who did that?"

"Both sides."

"That's nothing, Krantz, they did that in the Bible. 'Happy will they be who dash their little ones against the rock.'"

Ten thousand conversations. Breavman remembers about eight thousand of them. Peculiarities, horrors, wonders. They are still having them. As they grow older, the horrors become mental, the peculiarities sexual, the wonders religious.

And while they talked the car shot over the broken country roads and the All Night Record Man spun the disks of longing, and one by one the couples drove away from the Edgewater, the Maple Leaf, the El Paso. The dangerous currents of Lac St. Louis curled over the weekend's toll of drowned amateur sail-ors from the yacht clubs, the Montreal pioneer commuters breathed the cool fresh air they had bought into, and the pros-pect of waiting parents loomed and made the minutes of talk sweeter. Paradoxes, bafflements, problems dissolved in the fascinating dialectic.

Whoosh, there was nothing that couldn't be done.

25

Suspended from the centre of the ceiling a revolving mirrored sphere cast a rage of pockmarks from wall to wall of the huge Palais D'Or on lower Stanley Street.

Each wall looked like an enormous decayed Swiss cheese on the march.

On the raised platform a band of shiny-haired musicians sat behind heavy red and white music stands and blew the standard arrangements.

> *There's but one place for me*
> *Near you.*
> *It's like heaven to be*
> *Near you*

echoed coldly over the sparse dancers. Breavman and Krantz had got there too early. There was not much hope for magic.

"Wrong dance-hall, Breavman."

By ten o'clock the floor was jammed with sharply dressed couples, and, seen from the upstairs balcony, their swaying and jolting seemed to be nourished directly by the pulsing music, and they muffled it like shock absorbers. The bass and piano and steady brush-drum passed almost silently into their bodies where it was preserved as motion.

Only the tilt-backed trumpeter, arching away from the mike and pointing his horn at the revolving mirrored sphere, could put a lingering sharp cry in the smoky air, coiling like a rope of rescue above the bobbing figures. It disappeared as the chorus renewed itself.

"Right dance hall, Krantz."

They scorned many public demonstrations in those prowling days but they didn't scorn the Palais D'Or. It was too big.

There was nothing superficial about a thousand people deeply engaged in the courting ritual, the swinging fragments of reflected light sweeping across their immobile eye-closed faces, amber, green, violet. They couldn't help being impressed, fascinated by the channelled violence and the voluntary organization.

Why are they dancing to the music, Breavman wondered from the balcony, submitting to its dictation?

At the beginning of a tune they arranged themselves on the floor, obeyed the tempo, fast or slow. and when the tune was done they disintegrated into disorder again, like a battalion scattered by a land mine.

"What makes them listen, Krantz? Why don't they rip the platform to pieces?"

"Let's go down and get some women."

"Soon."

"What are you staring at?"

"I'm planning a catastrophe."

They watched the dancers silently and they heard their parents talking.

The dancers were Catholics, French-Canadian, anti-Semitic, anti-Anglais, belligerent. They told the priest everything, they were scared by the Church, they knelt in wax-smelling musty shrines hung with abandoned dirty crutches and braces. Everyone of them worked for a Jewish manufacturer whom he hated and waited for revenge. They had bad teeth because they lived on Pepsi-Cola and Mae West chocolate cakes. The girls were either maids or factory help. Their dresses were too bright and you could see bra straps through the flimsy material. Frizzy hair and cheap perfume. They screwed like jack rabbits and at confession the priest forgave them. They were the mob. Give them a chance and they'd burn down the synagogue. Pepsies. Frogs. Fransoyzen.

Breavman and Krantz knew their parents were bigots so they attempted to reverse all their opinions. They did not quite succeed. They wanted to participate in the vitality but they felt there was something vaguely unclean in their fun, the pawing of girls, the guffaws, the goosing.

The girls might be beautiful but they all had false teeth.

"Krantz, I believe we're the only two Jews in the place."

"No, I saw some BTOs on the make a couple of minutes ago."

"Well, we're the only Westmount Jews around."

"Bernie's here."

"O.K. Krantz, I'm the only Jew from Wellgreen Avenue. Do something with that."

"O.K. Breavman, you're the only Jew from Wellgreen Avenue at the Palais D'Or."

"Distinctions are important."

"Let's get some women."

At one of the doors in the main hall there was a knot of young people. They argued jovially in French, pushing one another, slapping back-sides, squirting Coke bottles.

The hunters approached the group and instantly modified its hilarity. The French boys stepped back slightly and Krantz and Breavman invited the girls they'd chosen. They spoke in French, fooling no one. The girls exchanged glances with each other and members of the party. One of the French boys magnanimously put his arm around the shoulder of the girl Breavman had asked and swept her to him, clapping Breavman on the back at the same time.

They danced stiffly. Her mouth was full of fillings. He knew he'd be able to smell her all night.

"Do you come here often, Yvette?"

"You know, once in a while, for fun."

"Me too. *Moi aussi.*"

He told her he was in high school, that he didn't work.

"You are Italian?"

"No."

"English?"

"I'm Jewish."

He didn't tell her he was the only one from Wellgreen Avenue.

"My brothers work for Jew people."

"Oh?"

"They are good to work for."

The dance was unsatisfying. She was not attractive, but her racial mystery challenged investigation. He returned her to her friends. Krantz had finished his dance, too.

"What was she like, Krantz?"

"Don't know. She couldn't speak English."

They hung around for a little while longer, drinking Orange Crush, leaning on the balcony rail to comment on the swaying mob below. The air was dense with smoke now. The band played either frantic jitterbug or slow fox trot, nothing between. After each dance the crowd hovered impatiently for the next one to begin.

It was late now. The wallflowers and the stag-line expected no miracles any more. They were lined along three walls watching the packed charged dancers with indifferent fixed stares. Some of the girls were collecting their coats and going home.

"Their new blouses were useless, Krantz."

Seen from above, the movement on the floor had taken on a frantic quality. Soon the trumpeter would aim his horn into the smoke and give the last of Hoagy Carmichael and it would be all over. Every throb of the band had to be hoarded now against the end of the evening and the silence. Soak it through pressed cheeks and closed eyes in the dreamy tunes. In the boogie-woogie gather the nourishment like manna and knead it between the bodies drawing away and towards each other.

"Let's get one more dance in, Breavman?"

"Same girls?"

"Might as well."

Breavman leaned over the rail one more second and wished he were delivering a hysterical speech to the thick mob below.

. . . and you must listen, friends, strangers, I am binding the generations one to another, o, little people of numberless streets, bark, bark, hoot, blood, your long stairways are curling around my heart like a vine . . .

They went downstairs and found the girls with the same group. It was a mistake, they knew instantly. Yvette stepped forward as if to tell Breavman something but one of the boys pulled her back.

"You like the girls, eh?" he said, the swaggerer of the party. His smile was triumphant rather than friendly.

"Sure we like them. Anything wrong with that?"

"Where you live, you?"

Breavman and Krantz knew what they wanted to hear. Westmount is a collection of large stone houses and lush trees arranged on the top of the mountain especially to humiliate the underprivileged.

"Westmount," they said with one voice.

"You have not the girls at Westmount, you?"

They had no chance to answer him. In the very last second before they fell backwards over the kneeling accomplices stationed behind them they detected a signalling of eyes. The ring-leader and a buddy stepped forward and shoved them. Breavman lost his balance and as he fell the stoolie behind him raised himself up to turn the fall into a flip. Breavman landed hard in a belly-flop, a couple of girls that he had crashed into squealing above him. He looked up to see Krantz on his feet, his left fist in someone's face and his right cocked back ready to fly. He was about to get up when a fat boy decided he shouldn't and dived at him.

"*Reste là, maudit juif!*"

Breavman struggled under the blankets of flesh, not trying to defeat the fat boy but merely to get out from under him so he could do battle from a more honourable upright position. He managed to squeeze away. Where was Krantz?

There must have been twenty people fighting. Here and there he could see girls on their tiptoes as though in fear of mice, while boys wrestled on the floor between them.

He wheeled around, expecting an attack. The fat boy was smothering someone else. He threw his fist at a stranger. He was a drop in the wave of history, anonymous, exhilarated, free.

"O, little friends, hoot, blooey, dark fighters, shazam, bloop!" he shouted in his happiness.

Racing down the stairs were three bouncers of the management's and what they feared most began to happen. The fighting spread to the dance floor. The band was blowing a loud dreamy tune but a disorganized noise could already be heard in opposition to the music.

Breavman waved his fist at everyone, hitting very few. The bouncers were in his immediate area, breaking up individual fights. At the far side of the hall the couples still danced closely and peacefully, but on Breavman's side their rhythm was disintegrating into flailing arms, blind punches, lunges, and female squeals.

The bouncers pursued the disruption like compulsive housekeepers after an enormous spreading stain, jerking fighters apart by their collars and sweeping them aside as they followed the struggle deeper into the dance floor.

A man rushed onto the bandstand and shouted something to the bandleader, who looked around and shrugged his shoulders. The bright lights went on and the curious coloured walls disappeared. The music stopped.

Everyone woke up. A noise like a wail of national mourning rose up and at the same time fighting swept over the hall like released entropic molecules. To see the mass of dancers change to mass of fighters was like watching a huge highly organized animal succumb to muscular convulsions.

Krantz grabbed Breavman.

"Mr. Breavman?"

"Krantzstone, I presume."

They headed for the front exit, which was already jammed with refugees. No one cared about his coat.

"Don't say it, Breavman."

"O.K. I won't say it, Krantz."

They got out just as the police arrived, about twenty of them in cars and the Black Maria. They entered with miraculous ease.

The boys waited in the front seat of the Lincoln. Krantz' jacket was missing a lapel. The Palais D'Or began to empty of its victims.

"Pity the guys in there, Breavman – and don't say it," he added quickly when he saw Breavman put on his mystical face.

"I won't say it, Krantz, I won't even whisper that I planned the whole thing from the balcony and executed it by the simple means of mass-hypnosis."

"You had to say it, eh?"

"We were mocked, Krantz. We seized the pillars and brought down the temple of the Philistines."

Krantz shifted into second with exaggerated weariness.

"Go on, Breavman. You have to say it."

26

He would love to have heard Hitler or Mussolini bellow from his marble balcony, to have seen partisans hang him upside down; to see the hockey crowds lynch the sports commissioner; to see the black or yellow hordes get even with the small outposts of their colonial enemies; to see the weeping country folk acclaim the strong-jawed road-builders; to see football fans rip down goal-posts; to have seen the panicking movie-viewers stampede Montreal children in the famous

re; to see five hundred thousand snap into any salute at all; to
ee a countless array of Arabian behinds pointing west; to see
he chalices on any altar tremble with the congregational
Amen.

And this is where he would like to be:

> in the marble balcony
> the press-box
> the projection-room
> the reviewing stand
> the minaret
> the Holy of Holies

And in each case he wants to be surrounded by the best
armed, squint-eyed, ruthless, loyal, tallest, leather-jacketed,
technical brain-washed heavy police guard that money can
buy.

27

Is there anything more beautiful than a girl with a lute?

It wasn't a lute. Heather, the Breavmans' maid, attempted
the ukulele. She came from Alberta, spoke with a twang, was
always singing laments and trying to yodel.

The chords were too hard. Breavman held her hand and
agreed that the strings were tearing her fingers to pieces. She
knew all the cowboy stars and traded their autographs.

She was a husky, good-looking girl of twenty with high-
coloured cheeks like a porcelain doll. Breavman chose her for
his first victim of sleep.

A veritable Canadian peasant.

He tried to make the offer attractive.

"You'll feel wonderful when you wake up."

Sure, she winked and settled herself on the couch in the
crammed basement store-room. If only it would work.

He moved his yellow pencil like a slow pendulum befor
her eyes.

"Your eyelids will feel heavy as lead on your cheeks. . . ."

He swung the pencil for ten minutes. Her large eyelid
thickened and slowed down. She followed the pencil with dif
ficulty.

"And your breathing heavy and regular. . . ."

Soon she let out a sigh, took in a deep breath, and breathe
like a drunkard, laboured and exhausted.

Now the eyelashes barely flickered. He couldn't believe tha
he had ordered the changes in her. Maybe she was joking.

"You're falling backwards, you're a tiny body falling back
wards, getting smaller and smaller, and you can hear nothin
but my voice. . . ."

Her breath was soft and he knew it would smell like wind.

He felt as though he had got his hands under her sweater
under her skin and ribs, and was manipulating her lungs, and
they felt like balloons of silk.

"You are asleep," he commanded in a whisper.

He touched her face in disbelief.

Was he really a master? She must be joking.

"Are you asleep?"

The yes came out the length of an exhalation, husky
unformed.

"You can feel nothing. Absolutely nothing. Do you under
stand?"

The same yes.

He drove a needle through the lobe of her ear. He was dizz
with his new power. All her energy at his disposal.

He wanted to run through the streets with a bell and sum
mon the whole cynical city. There was a new magician in th
world.

He had no interest in ears pierced by needles.

Breavman had studied the books. A subject cannot b
compelled to anything which he would consider indecen

while awake. But there were ways. For instance, a modest woman can be induced to remove her clothes before an audience of men if the operator can suggest a situation in which such an act can be performed quite naturally, such as taking a bath in the privacy of her own home, or a naked rest under the sun in some humid deserted place.

"It's hot, you've never been so hot. Your sweater weighs a ton. You're sweating like a pig. . . ."

As she undressed Breavman kept thinking of the illustrations in the pulp-paper Hypnotism for You manuals he knew by heart. Line drawings of fierce men leaning over smiling, sleeping women. Zigzags of electricity emanate from under the heavy eyebrows or from the tips of their piano-poised fingers.

Oh, she was, she really was, she was so lovely.

He had never seen a woman so naked. He ran his hand all over her body. He was astonished, happy, and frightened before all the spiritual authorities of the universe. He couldn't get it out of his mind that he was performing a Black Mass. Her breasts were strangely flat because she was lying on her back. The mound of her delta was a surprise and he cupped it in wonder. He covered her body with two trembling hands like mine-detectors. Then he sat back to stare, like Cortez over his new ocean. This was what he had waited for so long to see. He wasn't disappointed and never has been. The tungsten light was the same as the moon.

He unbuttoned his fly and told her she was holding a stick. His heart pounded.

He was intoxicated with relief, achievement, guilt, experience. There was semen on his clothes. He told Heather that the alarm clock had just rung. It was morning, she had to get up. He handed her her clothes and slowly she got dressed. He told her that she would remember nothing. Hurriedly he took her out of the sleep. He wanted to be alone and contemplate his triumph.

Three hours later he heard laughter from the basement and thought that Heather must be entertaining friends down there. Then he listened more carefully to the laughter and realized that it wasn't social.

He raced down the stairs. Thank God his mother was out. Heather was standing in the centre of the floor, legs apart, convulsed with frightened, hysterical laughter. Her eyes were rolled up in her head and shone white. Her head was thrown back and she looked as if she was about to fall over. He shook her. No response. Her laughter became a terrible fit of coughing.

I've driven her insane.

He wondered what the criminal penalty was. He was being punished for his illegal orgasm and his dark powers. Should he call a doctor, make his sin public right away? Would anyone know how to cure her?

He was close to panic as he led her to the couch and sat her down. Perhaps he should hide her in a closet. Lock her in a trunk and forget about everything. Those big steamers with his father's initials stencilled in white paint.

He slapped her face twice, once with each side of his hand, like a Gestapo investigator. She caught her breath, her cheek reddened and faded like a blush, and she spluttered again into cough-laughing. There was saliva on her chin.

"Be quiet, Heather!"

To his absolute surprise she stifled her cough.

It was then he realized that she was still hypnotized. He commanded her to lie down and close her eyes. He re-established contact with her. She was deep asleep. He had tried to bring her out too quickly and it hadn't taken. Slowly he worked her back to full wakefulness. She would be refreshed and gay. She would remember nothing.

This time she came round correctly. He chatted with her while just to make sure. She stood up with a puzzled look and patted her hips.

"Hey! My pants!"

Wedged between the couch and wall were her pink elastic-bottomed panties. He had forgotten to hand them to her when she was dressing.

Skilfully and modestly she slipped into them.

He waited for the unnatural punishment, the humiliation of the master, the collapse of his proud house.

"What have you been doing?" she said slyly, chucking him under the chin. "What went on while I was asleep? Eh? Eh?"

"What do you remember?"

She put her hands on her hips and smiled broadly at him.

"I'd never of thought it could be done. Never of thought."

"Nothing happened, Heather, I swear."

"And what would your mother say? Be looking for a job, I would."

She surveyed the couch and looked up at him with genuine admiration.

"Jewish people," she sighed. "Education."

Soon after his imaginary assault she ran off with a deserting soldier. He came alone for her clothes and Breavman watched with envy as he carried off her cardboard suitcase and unused ukulele. A week later Military Police visited Mrs. Breavman but she didn't know anything.

Where are you, Heather, why didn't you stay to introduce me into the warm important rites? I might have gone straight. Poemless, a baron of industry, I might have been spared the soft-cover books on rejection-level stabilization by wealthy New York analysts. Didn't you feel good when I brought you out?

Sometimes Breavman likes to think that she is somewhere in the world, not fully awake, sleeping under his power. And a man in a tattered uniform asks:

"Where are you, Heather?"

Book II

1

BREAVMAN LOVES the pictures of Henri Rousseau, the way he stops time.

Always is the word that must be used. The lion will always be sniffing the robes of the sleeping gypsy, there will be no attack, no guts on the sand: The total encounter is expressed. The moon, even though it is doomed to travel, will never go down on this scene. The abandoned lute does not cry for fingers. It is swollen with all the music it needs.

In the middle of the forest the leopard topples the human victim, who falls more slowly than the Tower of Pisa. He'll never reach the ground while you watch him, or even if you turn away. He is comfortable in his imbalance. The intricate leaves and limbs nourish the figures, not malignly or benignly, but naturally, as blossoms or fruits. But because the function is natural does not diminish its mystery. How have the animal flesh and the vegetable flesh become connected?

In another place the roots sponsor a wedding-couple or a family portrait. You are the photographer but you can never emerge from under the black hood or squeeze the rubber bulb or lose the image on the frosted glass. There is violence and immobility: the humans are involved, at home in each. It is not their forest, their clothes are city clothes, but the forest would be barren without them.

Wherever the violence or stillness happens, it is the centre of the picture, no matter how tiny or hidden. Cover it with your thumb and all the foliage dies.

2

In his first year of college, at a drinking place called the Shrine Breavman rose up with this toast:

"Jewish girls are not any more passionate than Gentile girls of any given economic area. Jewish girls have very bad legs. Of course, this is a generalization. In fact, the new American Jewess is being bred with long, beautiful legs.

"Negro girls are as screwed up as anyone else. They are no better than white girls, except, of course, the Anglo-Saxon girls from Upper Westmount, but even drugged sheep are better than they are. Their tongues are not rougher, nor is there any special quality in the lubricated areas. The second-to-best blow job in the world is a Negro girl I happen to know. She has a forty-seven thousand dollar mouth.

"The best blow job in the world (technically) is a French Canadian whore by the name of Yvette. Her telephone number is Château 2033. She has a ninety-thousand dollar mouth."

He raised high his cloudy glass.

"I am happy to give her the publicity here."

He sat down among the cheers of his comrades, suddenly tired of his voice. He had been expected for dinner but he hadn't phoned his mother. Obediently the new shot of Pernod turned white.

Krantz leaned over and whispered, "That was quite a speech for a sixteen-year-old virgin cherry to deliver upon us."

"Why didn't you pull me down?"

"They loved it."

"Why didn't you stop me?"

"Go stop you, Breavman."

"Let's get out of here, Krantz."

"Can you walk, Breavman?"

"No."

"Me neither. Let's go."

They supported each other through their favourite streets and alleys. They kept dropping their books and clip boards. They screamed hysterically at taxis that cruised too close. They tore up an economics text-book and burnt it as a sacrifice on the steps of a Sherbrooke Street bank. They prostrated themselves on the pavement. Krantz stood up first.

"Why aren't you praying, Krantz?"

"Car coming."

"Scream at it."

"Police car."

They ran down a narrow alley. A delicious smell stopped them, bestowed by the kitchen-ventilating fan of an expensive restaurant. They relieved themselves among the garbage cans.

"Breavman, you won't believe what I almost peed on."

"A corpse? A blonde wig? A full meeting of the Elders of Zion? An abandoned satchel of limp a-holes!"

"Shh. C'mere. Carefully."

Krantz lit a match and the brass eyes of a bull-frog gleamed from the debris. All three of them jumped at the same time. Krantz carried it in a knotted handkerchief.

"Must have escaped from a garlic sauce."

"Let's go back and liberate them all. Let the streets swarm with free frogs. Hey, Krantz, I've got my dissecting kit!"

They decided on a solemn ceremony at the foot of the War Memorial.

Breavman spread loose-leaf sheets on his Zoology text. He grasped the frog by the green hind legs. Krantz intervened, "You know, this is going to ruin the night. It's been a very fine night but this is going to ruin it."

"You're right, Krantz."

They stood there in silence. The night was immense. The

headlights streamed along Dorchester Street. They wishe
they weren't there, they wished they were at a party with
thousand people. The frog was as tempting to gut as an ol
alarm clock.

"Should I proceed, Krantz?"

"Proceed."

"We're in charge of torture tonight. The regular torture
are relieved."

Breavman swung the head smartly against the inscribe
stone. The smack of living tissue was louder than all the traffi

"At least that stuns it."

He laid the frog on the white sheets and secured it to th
book with pins through its extremities. He pierced the light
coloured abdomen with the scalpel. He withdrew the scissor
from his kit and made a long vertical incision in first the uppe
and then the lower layer of skin.

"We could stop now, Krantz. We could get thread an
repair the thing."

"We could," Krantz said dreamily.

Breavman pinned back the stretchy skin. They pressed i
over the deep insides, smelling each other's alcoholic breath

"This is the heart."

He lifted the organ with the small edge of the scalpel.

"So that's the heart."

The milky-grey sack heaved up and down and they stare
in wonder. The legs of the frog were like a lady's.

"I suppose I should get on with it."

He removed the organs one by one, the lungs, the kidney
A pebble and an undigested beetle were discovered in th
stomach. He exposed the muscles in the delicate thighs.

Both of them, the operator and the spectator, hovered in
trance. And finally he removed the heart, which alread
looked weary and ancient, the colour of old man's saliva, fir
heart of the world.

"If you put it in salt water it'll keep on beating for a while."

Krantz woke up.

"Will it? Let's do it. Hurry!"

Breavman tossed his text-book together with the emptied frog in a wire trash-basket as he ran. He cupped the heart in his hand, afraid of squeezing. The restaurant was only a minute away.

Don't die.

"Hurry! For Christ's sake!"

Everything had a second chance if they could save it.

They took a faraway booth in the bright restaurant. Where was the damn waitress?

"Look. It's still going."

Breavman placed it in a dish of warm salt water. It heaved its soft weight eleven more times. They counted each time and then said nothing for a while, their faces close to the table, immobile.

"It doesn't look like anything now," Breavman said.

"What's a dead frog's heart supposed to look like?"

"I suppose that's the way everything evil happens, like tonight."

Krantz grabbed his shoulder, his face suddenly bright.

"That's brilliant, what you just said is brilliant!"

He slapped his friend's back resoundingly. "You're a genius, Breavman!"

Breavman was puzzled at Krantz's tangent from depression. He silently reconstructed his remark.

"You're right! Krantz, you're right! And so are you – for noticing it!"

They seized each other's shoulders and pounded each other's backs over the Arborite table, bellowing compliments and congratulations.

"You genius!"

"*You* genius!"

They spilled the salt water, not that it mattered. They turned over the table. They were geniuses! They knew how it happens.

The manager wanted to know if they'd like to get out.

3

The heavy gold frame of his father's picture was the first thing he noticed. It seemed like another window.

"You're wasting your life in bed, you're turning night into day," his mother shouted outside the door.

"Will you leave me alone? I just got up."

He stared for a long while at his bookshelf, watching the sun move from the leather Chaucer to the leather Wordsworth. Good sun, in harmony with history. Comforting thought for early morning. Except that it is the middle of the afternoon.

"How can you waste your life in bed? How can you do this to me?"

"I'm on a different cycle. I go to bed late. Please go away."

"The beautiful sun. You're ruining your health."

"I still sleep my seven hours, it's just that I sleep them at a different time than you sleep yours."

"The beautiful sun," she wailed, "the park, you could be walking."

What am I doing arguing with her?

"But mother, I walked in the park last night. It was still the park then, in the night."

"You turn night into day, you're using up your time, your beautiful health."

"Leave me alone!"

She's in bad shape, she just wants to talk, she'll use any maternal duty as an occasion for lengthy debate.

He rested his elbows on the window sill and let the landscape develop in his thought. Park. Lilacs. Nurses in white talking together beside the green branches or pushing dark carriages. Children launching their white sailboats from the concrete shore of the blue pool, praying for wind, safe journeys or spectacular wrecks.

"What do you want for your brunch? Eggs, scrambled, salmon, there's a lovely piece of steak, I'll tell her to make you a salad, what do you want in it, Russian dressing, how do you want your eggs, there's coffee-cake, fresh, the refrigerator is full, in this house there is always something to eat, nobody goes hungry, thank God, there are oranges imported from California, do you want juice?"

He opened the door and spoke carefully.

"I'm aware how fortunate we are. I'll take some juice when I feel like it. Don't disturb the maid or anybody."

But she was already at the banister, shouting, "Mary, Mary, prepare Mr. Lawrence some orange juice, squeeze three oranges. How do you want your eggs, Lawrence?"

She slipped the last question to him like a trick.

"Will you stop shoving food down my throat? You can make a person sick with your damn food!"

He slammed his door.

"He slams a door at a mother," she reported bitterly from the hall.

What a mess! His clothes were everywhere. His desk was a confusion of manuscripts, books, underwear, fragments of Eskimo sculpture. He tried to shove a half-finished sestina into the drawer but it was jammed with accumulated scraps, boarded envelopes, abandoned diaries.

What this room needs is a good, clean fire. He couldn't find his kimono so he covered himself with *The New York Times* and ran across the hall into the bathroom.

"Very pretty. He wears a newspaper."

He managed to creep downstairs, but his mother ambushed him in the kitchen.

"Is that all you're having, orange juice, with the house filled with food, half the world fighting for leftovers?"

"Don't start, Mother."

She threw open the door of the refrigerator.

"Look," she challenged. "Look at all this, eggs that you didn't want, look at the size of them, cheese, Gruyère, Oka, Danish, Camembert, some cheese and crackers. and who's going to drink all the wine, that's a shame, Lawrence, look at them, feel the weight of this grapefruit, we're so lucky, and meat, three kinds, I'll make it myself, feel the weight. . . ."

Try and see the poem, Breavman, the beautiful catalogue.

"– here, feel the weight. . . ."

He heaved the raw slab of steak at her feet, splitting the wax-paper on the linoleum.

"Haven't you got anything better to do with your life than stuff food down my face? I'm not starving."

"This is the way a son talks to his mother," she informed the world.

"Will you leave me alone now?"

"This is a son talking, your father should see you, he should be here to see you throwing down meat, meat on the floor, what tyrant does that, only someone rotten, to do this to a mother. . . ."

He followed her out of the kitchen.

"I just asked to be left alone, to wake up by myself."

"Rotten, a rat wouldn't treat a mother, rotten as if you were a stranger, would anybody throw meat and my ankles are swollen, beat you, your father would beat you, a rotten son. . . ."

He followed her up the stairs.

"You can make someone sick with your screaming."

She slammed her closet door. He stood beside it and listened to her opening and shutting the big drawers.

"Get away! A son talks to a mother, a son can kill a mother, I knew everything, what I have to hear, a traitor not a son, to talk to me, nobody who remembers me to talk. . . ."

He heard her slide open the dress compartment. First she tore the sleeves from some old housecoats. She tripped over a tangle of hangers. Then she began on an expensive black one she had bought in New York.

"What good are they, what good are they, when a son is killing a mother. . . ."

He heard every sound, his cheek pressed against the wood.

4

At night the park was his domain.

He covered all the playing fields and hills like a paranoiac squire hunting for poachers. The flower-beds, the terraces of grass had an aspect of formality they did not have by daylight. The trees were taller and older. The high-fenced tennis court looked like a cage for huge wingless creatures which had somehow got away. The ponds were calm and deadly black. Lamps floated in them like multiple moons.

Walking past the Chalet he remembered the masculine smell of hockey equipment and underwear, the thud of skates on wooden planks.

The empty baseball diamond was blurred with spectacular sliding ghosts. He could hear the absence of cheers. With no bikes leaning against them the chestnut tree and wire backstop seemed strangely isolated.

How many leaves have to scrape together to record the rustle of the wind? He tried to distinguish the sound of acacia from the sound of maple.

Just beyond the green rose the large stone houses of Westmount Avenue. In them the baseball players were growing their bodies with sleep, resting their voices. He imagined that he could see them dimly through the walls of the upper storeys, or rather the sheets they were wrapped in, floating row upon row over the street, like a colony of cocoons in a moonlit tree. The young men of his age, Christian and blond, dreaming of Jewish sex and bank careers.

The park nourished all the sleepers in the surrounding houses. It was the green heart. It gave the children dangerous bushes and heroic landscapes so they could imagine bravery. It gave the nurses and maids winding walks so they could imagine beauty. It gave the young merchant-princes leaf-hid necking benches, views of factories so they could imagine power. It gave the retired brokers vignettes of Scottish lanes where loving couples walked, so they could lean on their canes and imagine poetry. It was the best part of everyone's life. Nobody comes into a park for mean purposes except perhaps a sex maniac and who is to say that he isn't thinking of eternal roses as he unzips before the skipping-rope Beatrice?

He visited the Japanese pond to ensure the safety of the goldfish. He climbed through the prickly bushes and over the wall to inspect the miniature waterfall. Lisa was not there. He somersaulted down the hill to see if it was still steep enough. Wouldn't it be funny if Lisa of all people should be waiting at the bottom? He sifted a handful in the sand-box to guard against polio. He did a test run on the slide, surprised that it squeezed him. He looked gravely from the lookout to guarantee the view.

"My city, my river, my bridges, shit on you, no I didn't mean it."

The bases had to be run, the upper ponds examined for sail-boat wrecks or abandoned babies or raped white nurses. Touch the tree trunks to encourage them.

He had his duty to the community, to the nation.

At any moment a girl is going to step out of one of the flower-beds. She will look as though she has just been swimming and she'll know all about my dedication.

He lay under the lilacs. The flowers were almost gone, they looked like molecular diagrams. Sky was immense. Cover me with black fire. Uncles, why do you look so confident when you pray? Is it because you know the words? When the curtains of the Holy Ark are drawn apart and gold-crowned Torah scrolls revealed, and all the men of the altar wear white clothes, why don't your eyes let go of the ritual, why don't you succumb to raving epilepsy? Why are your confessions so easy?

He hated the men floating in sleep in the big stone houses. Because their lives were ordered and their rooms tidy. Because they got up every morning and did their public work. Because they weren't going to dynamite their factories and have naked parties in the fire.

There were lights on the St. Lawrence the size of stars, and an impatient stillness in the air. Trees as fragile as the legs of listening deer. At any minute the sun would come crashing out of the roofs like a clenched fist, driving out determined workers and one-way cars to jam the streets. He hoped he wouldn't have to see the herds of traffic on Westmount Avenue. Turning night into day.

"Hello there."

A stout man of thirty in an Air Force uniform stood above him. He had been the centre of attention in the park a few days before. Several nurses complained that he had been too enthusiastic in the fondling of their male children. A policeman had escorted him to the street and invited him to move along.

"I thought you weren't allowed in here."

"Nobody's around. I just felt like talking."

His uniform was sharply pressed. Really, he was too clean for that time of the morning or night or whatever it was. Breavman isolated the smell of shaving lotion from the lilac-laden air. He stood up.

"Talk. You have my permission. I'm going home."

"I just thought . . ."

Breavman looked back over his shoulder and shouted, "Talk! Why aren't you talking? It's all yours – the park's empty!"

There were gardeners in faded clothes on his street. They called to one another as they swept, all Italian names. Breavman studied their brooms made out of wire-bound branches. It must be nice to use something that real.

5

"Will you stop shouting, Breavman, or stand further back, I can't hear a damn thing you're saying."

"Bertha, I said! I just saw Bertha! She's in town!"

"Bertha who?"

"Oh, you wicked and careless fool. Bertha of our childhood, of The Tree, who mangled herself under our noses."

"How does she look?"

"Her face is perfect, really Krantz, she was beautiful."

"Where did you see her?"

"In a bus window."

"Good-bye, Breavman."

"Don't hang up, Krantz. I swear it was really her. I won't say she was smiling. It was an open, blonde face with no family lines, so you could make anything you want of it."

"You go follow the bus, Breavman."

"Oh, no, she saw me. I'll just wait here till it comes round again. She moved her lips."

"Good-bye, Breavman."

"Krantz, this is a most pleasant telephone booth I'm living in today. Sherbrooke Street is a parade of everyone I ever knew. I'm going to loiter immoderately. They'll all be delivered to me today, Bertha, Lisa. Nobody, not one name, not one limb will be taken away in the dustload."

"Where did you dig up those old names?"

"I'm the keeper. I'm the sentimental dirty old man in front of a classroom of children."

"Good-bye, Breavman, for real."

It was a beautiful telephone box. It smelled of new spring paint and fresh nails. You could feel the sun through the wire-embedded glass. He was the guard, he was the sentry.

Bertha, who had fallen out of a tree for his sake! Bertha, who played "Greensleeves" sweeter than he ever could! Bertha, who fell with apples and twisted her limbs!

He dropped in another nickel and waited for the music.

"Krantz, she just came round again. . . ."

6

Wait, wait, wait, wait. Everything took so long.

The mountain released the moon like a bubble it could no longer contain, with reluctance and pain.

That summer Breavman had a queer sense of time slowing down.

He was in a film and the machine was whirring into slower and slower motion.

Eight years later he told Shell about it, but not everything, because he didn't want Shell to think that he saw her in the same way he saw the girl he was telling about, as if she were a moon-lit body in a slow Swedish movie, and from far away.

What was her name? he demanded of himself.

I forget. It was a sweet, Jewish last name which meant mother-of-pearl or rose-forest.

How dare you forget?

Norma.

What did she look like?

It doesn't matter what she looked like every day. It only

matters what she looked like for that important second. That I remember and will tell you.

What did she look like every day?

As a matter of fact, her face was squashed, her nose spread too wide. One of her grandmothers must have been carried away by the Tartars. She always seemed to be astride something, a railing or a diving-board, waving her brown arms, eyes lost in her laugh, galloping to a feast or a massacre. Her flesh was loose.

Why was she a Communist?

Because she played the guitar. Because the copper bosses shot Joe Hill. Because *no tenemos ni aviones ni cañones,* and all her friends had died at Jarama. Because General MacArthur was a criminal and ruled Japan as a personal kingdom. Because the Wobblies sang into tear gas. Because Sacco loved Vanzetti. Because Hiroshima hurt her eyes and she was collecting names on a Ban the Bomb petition and was often told to go back to Russia.

Did she limp?

When she was very tired you noticed it. She usually wore a long Mexican skirt.

And the Mexican ring?

Yes, she was engaged to a chartered accountant. She assured me that he was progressive. But how could someone who was waiting for a revolution be a chartered accountant? I wanted to know. And how could she, with her ideas of freedom, commit herself to conventional marriage?

"We have to be effective in society. Communists aren't bohemians. That's a luxury of Westmount."

Did you love her?

I loved to kiss her breasts, the few times she let me.

How many times, how many times?

Twice. And I was allowed to touch. Arms, stomach, pubic hair, I almost made the jewel of my list but her jeans were too tight. She was four years older than me.

She was engaged?

But I was young. She kept telling me I was a baby. So nothing we did was really important. She phoned him long distance every night. I stood beside her as she spoke. They talked about apartments and wedding plans. It was the prosaic adult world, the museum of failure, and I had nothing to do with it.

What about her face when she talked to him?

I believe I could read guilt on it.

Liar.

We both felt terribly guilty, I guess. So we worked hard to collect more signatures. But we loved to lie together beside the fire. Our tiny circle of light seemed so far from everything. I told her stories. She made up a blues called *"My Golden Bourgeois Baby Sold His House For Me."* No, that's a lie.

What did you do during the day?

We hitch-hiked all over the Laurentians. We'd go down to a beach crowded with sun-bathers and we'd start singing. We were brown, we had good harmonies, people liked to listen to us even if they didn't open their eyes. Then I'd talk.

"I'm not talking about Russia or America. I'm not even talking about politics. I'm talking about your bodies, the ones stretched out on this beach, the ones you've just smeared with sun-tan oil. Some of you are over-weight and some of you are too thin, and some of you are very proud. You all know your bodies. You've looked at them in mirrors, you've waited to hear them complimented, or touched with love. Do you want what you kiss to turn to cancer? Do you want to take handfuls of hair from your child's scalp? You see, I'm not talking about Russia or America. I'm talking about bodies, which are all we have, and no government can restore one finger, one tooth, one inch of normal skin that is lost because of the poison in the air. . . ."

Did they listen?

They listened and most of them signed. I knew I could be Prime Minister because of the way their eyes listened. It didn't matter what was said as long as the old words were used and the old chanting rhythm, I could have led them into a drowning ritual. . . .

Stop this fantasy right now. What were the bodies like on the beach?

Ugly and white and ruined by offices.

What did you do at night?

She helped me to her bare breasts and the clothed outline of her body.

Be more specific, will you?

The mountain released the moon, like a bubble it could no longer contain, with reluctance and pain. I was in a film and the machine was whirring into slower and slower motion.

A bat swooped over the fire and thudded into the pines. Norma closed her eyes and pressed the guitar closer. She sent a minor chord through his spine and into the forest.

America was lost, the scabs ruled everything, the skyscrapers of chrome would never budge, but Canada was here, infant dream, the stars high and sharp and cold, and the enemies were brittle and easy and English.

The firelight grazed over her, calling out a cheek, a hand, then waving it back to the darkness.

The camera takes them from faraway, moves through the forest, catches the glint of a raccoon's eyes, examines the water, reeds, closed water-flowers, involves itself with mist and rocks.

"Lie beside me," Norma's voice, maybe Breavman's.

Sudden close-up of her body part by part, lingering over the mounds of her thighs, which are presented immense and shadowed, the blue denim tight on the flesh. The fan of creases between her thighs. Camera searches her jacket for the shape of breasts. She exhumes a pack of cigarettes. Activity is studied closely. Her fingers move like tentacles. Manipulation of cigarette skilled and suggestive. Fingers are slow, violent, capable of holding anything.

He flicks his sight like a dry fly and whips back the shape he's caught. She makes an O of her mouth and pushes out a smoke ring with her tongue.

"Let's go swimming."

They stand, they walk, they collide in a loud rush of clothing. Face each other with eyes closed. Camera holds each face, one after the other. They kiss blindly, missing mouths, finding them wet. They fall into a noise of crickets and breathing.

"No, this is too serious now."

Camera records them lying in silence.

There are distances between each word.

"Then let's go swimming."

Camera follows them to the shore. They go through the woods with difficulty, the audience has forgotten where they are going, it takes so long, the branches will not let them by.

"Oh, let me see you."

"I'm not so pretty underneath. You stand over there."

She moves to the other side of an orchard of reeds and now they cross every picture like lines of rain. The moon is a shore-stone someone lucky has found.

So she emerges wet, her skin tightened by gooseflesh, and the whole bright screen enfolds him, lenses and machinery.

"No, don't touch me. It's not so bad then. Don't move. I've never done this to anyone."

Her hair was wet on his stomach. His mind broke into postcards.

Dear Krantz

What she did what she did what she did

Dear Bertha

You must limp like her or maybe even look like I knew nothing was lost

Dear Hitler

Take away the torches I'm not guilty I had to have this

"Will you walk me down to the village? I promised I'd telephone and it must be late."

"You're not going to phone him *now*?"

"I said I would."

"But after this?"

She touched his cheek. "You know that I have to."

"I'll wait at the fire."

When she was gone he folded his sleeping bag. He couldn't find his right moccasin but that didn't matter. Sticking out of her kit-bag he noticed a packet of Ban the Bomb petition forms. He crouched beside the fire and scribbled signatures.

> I. G. Farben
> Mister Universe
> Joe Hill
> Wolfgang Amadeus Jolson
> Ethel Rosenberg
> Uncle Tom
> Little Boy Blue
> Rabbi Sigmund Freud.

He shoved the forms down her sleeping bag and headed for the highway, which was streaked with headlights. *Nothing could help the air.*

What did she look like that important second?

She stands in my mind alone, unconnected to the petty narrative. The colour of the skin was startling, like the white of a young branch when the green is thumb-nailed away. Nipples the colour of bare lips. Wet hair a battalion of glistening spears laid on her shoulders.

She was made of flesh and eyelashes.

But you said she was lame, perhaps like Bertha would be from the fall?

I don't know.

Why can't you tell Shell?

My voice would depress her.

Shell touched Breavman's cheek.

"Tell me the rest of the story."

7

Tamara had long legs, God knows how long they were. Sometimes at the meetings she used up three chairs. Her hair was tangled and black. Breavman tried to select one coil and follow where it fell and weaved. It made his eyes feel as though he had walked into a closet of dustless cobwebs.

Breavman and Krantz wore special costumes for hunting Communist women. Dark suits, vests which buttoned high on their shirts, gloves and umbrellas.

They attended every meeting of the Communist Club. They sat imperially among the open-collared members who were munching their sandwich lunches out of paper bags.

During a dull speech on American germ-warfare Krantz whispered: "Breavman, why are paper bags full of white bread so ugly?"

"I'm glad you asked, Krantz. They are advertisements for the frailty of the body. If a junkie wore his hypodermic needle pinned to his lapel you'd feel exactly the same disgust. A bag bulging with food is a kind of visible bowel. Trust the Bolsheviks to wear their digestive systems on their sleeves!"

"Sufficient, Breavman. I thought you'd know."

"Look at her, Krantz!"

Tamara appropriated another chair for her mysterious limbs. At the same moment the chairman interrupted the speaker and waved his gavel at Krantz and Breavman.

"If you two jokers don't shut up you're getting right out of here."

They stood up to make a formal apology.

"Siddown, siddown, just keep quiet."

Korea had swarmed with Yankee insects. They had bombs filled with contagious mosquitoes.

"Now I have some questions for you, Krantz. What goes on under those peasant blouses and skirts she always wears? How high do her legs go up? What happens after her wrists plunge into her sleeves? Where do her breasts begin?"

"That's why you're here, Breavman."

Tamara had gone to his high-school but he didn't notice her then because she was fat. They took the same route to school, but he never noticed her. Lust was training his eyes to exclude everything he could not kiss.

But now she was slender and tall. Her ripe lower lip curved over its own little shadow. She moved heavily, though, as if her limbs were still bound with the mass of flesh she remembered with bitterness.

"Do you know one of the main reasons why I want her?"

"I know the main reason."

"You're wrong, Krantz. It's because she lives one street away from me. She belongs to me for the same reason the park does."

"You're a very sick boy."

A minute later Krantz said: "These people are half right about you, Breavman. You're an emotional imperialist."

"You thought about that for a long time, didn't you?"

"A while."

"It's good."

They shook hands solemnly. They exchanged umbrellas. They tightened each other's ties. Breavman kissed Krantz on each cheek in the manner of a French general awarding medals.

The chairman hammered his gavel to preserve the meeting.

"Out! We're not interested in a vaudeville show. Go perform on the mountain!"

The mountain meant Westmount. They decided to accept his advice. They practised a soft-shoe routine at the Lookout, delighting in their own absurdity. Breavman never could master the steps, but he liked swinging the umbrella.

"Do you know why I love Communist women?"

"I do, Breavman."

"You're wrong again. It's because they don't believe in the world."

They sat on the stone wall, their backs to the river and city.

"Very soon, Krantz, very soon I'm going to be in a room with her. We're going to be in a room. There's going to be a room around us."

"So long, Breavman, I've got to study."

Krantz's house wasn't far. He meant it, he really went. It was the first time Krantz had –

"Hey!" Breavman called. "You broke the dialogue."

He was out of hearing.

8

"Don't you see it, Tamara, don't you see that both sides, both sides of every fight, they're both always using germ-warfare?"

He was walking with her in the park behind his house, telling the secret of conflict and the habits of nocturnal goldfish and why poets are the unacknowledged legislators of the world.

Then he was in a room undressing her. He couldn't believe his hands. The kind of surprise when the silver paper comes off the triangle of Gruyère in one piece.

Then she said no and bundled her clothes against her breasts.

He felt like an archaeologist watching the sand blow back. She was putting on her bra. He helped her with the clasp just to show that he wasn't a maniac.

Then he asked why four times.

Then he stood at the window.

Tell her you love her, Breavman. That's what she wants to hear. He came back and rubbed her back.

Now he was working in the small of her back.

Say I love you. Say it. One-two-three, now.

He was getting an occasional finger under the elastic.

She crossed her ankles and seemed to squeeze her thighs together in some kind of private pleasure. This gesture shivered his spine.

Then he dived at her thighs, which were floating and damp. The flesh splashed up. He used his teeth. He didn't know whether the wetness was blood or spit or lubricating perfume.

Then there were the strange strained voices which had turned into whispers, rushed and breathless, as though time were against them, bringing police and parents to the keyhole.

"I better put something on."

"I'm afraid I'm tight."

"It's beautiful that you're tight."

Who was she, who owned her body?

"You see, I'm tight."

"Oh yes."

Congratulations, like slow-falling confetti, covered his mind with sleep, but someone said: "Tell me a poem."

"Let me look at you first."

"Let me look at you too."

Then he walked her home. It was his personal time of the morning. The sun was threatening in the east. The newsboys were limping with their grey bags. The sidewalks looked new.

Then he took her hands in his hands and spoke with serious appreciation:

"Thank you, Tamara."

Then she slapped his face with the hand that was holding the key.

"It sounds so horrible. As if I let you take something. As if you got something out of me."

She cried for the seconds it took until a line of blood appeared on his cheek.

Then they hugged to repair everything.

When she was inside she put her mouth to the window of the door and they kissed through the glass. He wanted her to go first and she wanted him to go first. He hoped his back looked good.

C'mon, everybody! He exulted as he marched home, newest member of the adult community. Why weren't all the sleepers hanging out of their windows cheering? Didn't they admire his ritual of love and deceit? He visited his park, stood on the nursery hill and looked over the city to the grey river. He was finally involved with the sleepers, the men who went to work, the buildings, the commerce.

Then he threw stones at Krantz's window because he didn't want to go to bed.

"Steal a car, Krantz. Chinese soup time."

Breavman told everything in three minutes and then they drove in silence. He leaned his head against the window glass expecting it to be cool, but it wasn't.

"I know why you're depressed. Because you told me."

"Yes. I dishonoured it twice."

It was worse than that. He wished he loved her, it must be so nice to love her, and to tell her, not once or five times, but over and over, because he knew he was going to be with her in rooms for a long time.

Then what about rooms, wasn't every room the same, hadn't he known what it would be like, weren't all the rooms they passed exactly the same, wherever a woman was stretched out, even a forest was a glass room, wasn't it like with Lisa, under the bed and when they played the Soldier and the Whore, wasn't it the same, even to the listening for enemy sounds?

He told the story again, six years later, to Shell, but he didn'
dishonour it that time. Once, when he went away from She
for a little while, he wrote her this:

"I think that if Elijah's chariot, or Apollo's, or any mythica
boat of the sky, should pull up at my doorstep, I would know
exactly where to sit, and as we flew I'd recall with deliciou
familiarity all the clouds and mysteries we passed."

9

Tamara and Breavman rented a room in the east end of th
city. They told their families they were visiting out-of-town
friends.

"I'm used to being alone," his mother said.

On the last morning they leaned out of the small high win
dow, squashing shoulders, looking at the street below.

Alarms went off through the boarding house. Bulging ash
cans sentried the dirty sidewalk. Cats cruised between them

"You won't believe this, Tamara, but there was a time
could have frozen one of those cats to the sidewalk."

"That's very useful, frozen cat."

"I can't make things happen so easily these days, alas
Things happen to *me*. I couldn't even hypnotize you las
night."

"You're a failure, Larry, but I'm still crazy about your balls
Yummy."

"My lips are sore from kissing."

"So are mine."

They kissed softly and then she touched his lips with he
hand. She was often very tender and it always surprised hin
because he hadn't commanded it.

They had hardly been out of bed for the past five days. Even
with the window wide open, the air in the room smelt like th
bed. The early-morning buildings filled him with nostalgi

nd he couldn't understand it until he realized that they were
xactly the colour of old tennis shoes.

She rubbed her shoulder against his chin to feel the bristle.
Ie looked at her face. She had closed her eyes to savour the
norning breeze against her eyelids.

"Cold?"

"Not if you stay."

"Hungry?"

"I couldn't face another anchovy and that's all we have."

"We shouldn't have bought such expensive stuff. It doesn't
quite go with the room, does it?"

"Neither do we," she said. "Everybody in the house seems
o be getting up for work."

"And here we are: refugees from Westmount. You've
petrayed your new socialist heritage."

"You can talk all you want if you let me smell you."

The cigarettes were crushed. He straightened one out and
it it for her. She blew a mouthful of smoke into the morning.

"Smoking with nothing on is so – so luxurious."

She shivered over the word. He kissed the nape of her neck
and they resumed their idle watch in the window.

"Cold?"

"I'd like to stay for a year," she said.

"That's called marriage."

"Now don't get all frightened and prickly."

A very important thing happened.

They caught sight of an old man in an oversize raincoat
standing in a doorway across the street, pressed against the
door as if he were hiding.

They decided to watch him, just to see what he did.

He leaned forward, looked up and down the street, and
satisfied that it was empty, gathered the folds of his raincoat
around him like a cape and stepped out on the sidewalk.

Tamara flicked a roll of ashes out the window. It fell like a feather and then disintegrated in the rising wind. Breavman watched the small gesture.

"I can't stand how beautiful your body is."

She smiled and leaned her head against his shoulder.

The old man in the swaddling coat kneeled and peered under a parked car. He got up, brushed his knees, and looked around.

The wind moved in her hair, detaching and floating a wisp. She squeezed her arm between them and flicked the butt. He flicked his out too. They fell like tiny doomed parachutists.

Then, as if the butts were a signal, everything began to happen faster.

The sun jelled suddenly between two buildings, intensely darkening the charade of chimneys.

A citizen climbed into his car and drove away.

A cat appeared a few feet from where the old man was standing and crossed in front of him, proud, starved, and muscular. With a flurry of folds the old man leaped after the animal. Effortlessly, the cat changed its direction and softly padded down stone stairs to a cellar entrance. The man coughed and followed, stooped, baffled, and climbed back to the street empty-handed.

They had watched him idly, as people watch water, but now they looked hard.

"You've got gooseflesh, Tamara."

She refastened a wisp of floating hair. He studied her fingers in the exercise. He remembered them on various parts of his body.

He thought he would be content if he were condemned to live that moment over and over for the rest of his life. Tamara naked and young, her fingers weaving a lock of hair. The sun tangled in TV aerials and chimneys. The morning breeze whipping the mist from the mountain. A mysterious old man whose mystery he didn't care to learn. Why should he go looking for better visions?

He couldn't make things happen.

In the street the old man was lying on his stomach under the bumper of a car, grasping after a cat he had managed to corner between the kerb and the wheel. He kicked his feet in excitement, trying to get the cat by the hind legs, getting scratched and nipped. He finally succeeded. He extracted the cat from the shadows and held it above his head.

The cat wriggled and convulsed like a pennant in a violent wind.

"My God," said Tamara. "What's he doing with it?"

They forgot each other and leaned out the window.

The old man staggered under the struggle of the big cat, his face buried in his chest away from the threshing claws. He regained his footing. Wielding the cat as if it were an axe, his feet spread wide, he brought it down hard against the sidewalk. They could hear the head smash from their window. It convulsed like a landed fish.

Tamara turned her head away.

"What's he doing now?" she wanted to be told.

"He's putting it in a bag."

The old man, kneeling beside the twitching cat, had produced a paper bag from out of his huge coat. He attempted to stuff the cat into it.

"I'm sick," said Tamara. She was hiding her face against his chest. "Can't you do something?"

It hadn't occurred to Breavman that he could intrude into the action.

"Hey you!"

The old man looked up suddenly.

"*Oui! Toi!*"

The old man stopped short. He looked down at his cat. His hands vibrated in indecision. He fled down the street coughing and empty-handed.

Tamara gurgled. "I'm going to be sick." She broke for the sink and vomited.

Breavman helped her to the bed.

"Anchovies," she said.

"You're shivering. I'll close the window."

"Just lie beside me."

Her body was limp as though it had succumbed to som defeat. It frightened him.

"Maybe we shouldn't have frightened him off," he said.

"What do you mean?"

"He was probably starving."

"He was going to *eat* it?"

"Well, we protected our fragile tastes."

She held him tightly. It was not the kind of embrace h wanted. There was nothing of flesh in it, only hurt.

"We didn't sleep very much. Try to sleep now."

"Will you sleep too?"

"Yes. We're both tired."

The morning world had been removed from them, th jagged sounds of traffic were beyond the closed window, dis tant as history. They were two people in a room and there wa nothing to watch.

With his hand he soothed her hair and closed her eyelid He remembered the miniature work of the wind unfastenin and floating wisps of hair. A week is a long time.

Her lips trembled.

"Lawrence?"

I know what you're going to say and I know what I'm goin to say and I know what you're going to say. . . .

"Don't be mad."

"No."

"I love you," she said simply.

I'll wait here.

"You don't have to say anything," she said.

"Thank you," he said.

"Will you kiss me?"

He kissed her mouth lightly.

"Are you angry with me?"

"What do you mean?" he lied.

"For what I said. I know it hurts you in some way."

"No, Tamara, it makes me feel close to you."

"I'm happy I told you."

She adjusted her position and moved closer to him, not for sensation but for warmth and protection. He held her tightly, not as mistress, but bereaved child. The room was hot. Sweat on his palms.

Now she was asleep. He made sure she was asleep. Carefully he disengaged himself from her hold. If only she weren't so beautiful in sleep. How could he run from that body?

He dressed like a thief.

A round sun burned above the sooty buildings. All the parked cars had driven away. A few old men, brooms in hand, stood blinking among the garbage cans. One of them tried to balance the cat's carcass on a broom handle because he didn't want to touch it.

Run, Westmount, run.

He needed to put distance between himself and the hot room where he couldn't make things happen. Why did she have to speak? Couldn't she have left it alone? The smell of her flesh was trapped in his clothes.

Her body was with him and he let a vision of it argue against his flight.

I am running through a snowfall which is her thighs, he dramatized in purple. Her thighs are filling up the street. Wide as a snowfall, heavy as huge falling Zeppelins, her damp thighs are settling on the sharp roofs and wooden balconies. Weather-vanes press the shape of roosters and sail-boats into the skin. The faces of famous statues are preserved like intaglios. . . .

Then he was thinking of a special pair of thighs in a special room. Commitment was oppressive but the thought of flesh-loneliness was worse.

Tamara was awake when he opened the door. He undressed in a hurry and renewed what he had nearly lost.

"Aren't you glad you came back?"

For three years Tamara was his mistress, until he was twenty.

10

In the third year of college Breavman left his house. He and Krantz took a couple of rooms downtown on Stanley Street.

When Breavman informed his mother that he intended to spend several nights a week downtown she seemed to accept the fact calmly.

"You can use a toaster, can't you. We have an extra toaster."

"Thank you, Mother."

"And cutlery, you'll need cutlery."

"Not really, we're not going to do any serious cooking. . . ."

"You'll need plenty of cutlery, Lawrence."

She went from drawer to drawer in the kitchen selecting items and heaping them on the table before him.

"Mother, I don't need an egg-beater."

"How do you know?"

She emptied a drawer of silver fish forks on the table. She struggled with the string drawer but she couldn't get it out.

"Mother, this is ridiculous."

"Take everything."

He followed her into the living-room. Now she was above him, tottering in a soft chair, trying to keep her balance, while at the same time unhooking some heavy embroidered curtains.

"What are you doing?"

"What do I need in an empty house? Take everything!"

She kicked the fallen curtains towards him and tripped in the folds. Breavman ran to help her. She seemed so heavy.

"Get away, what do I need, take everything!"

"Stop this, Mother, please."

On the way up the stairs she tore a Persian miniature mounted on velvet from its hook and thrust it at him.

"You have walls down there, don't you?"

"Please go to bed, Mother."

She began to empty the linen closet, heaving piles of sheets and blankets at his feet. Standing on tip-toe she tugged at a stack of tablecloths. One unfolded as she pulled and fell about her like a ghost's costume. She thrashed inside it. He tried to help her but she fought him from under the linen.

He stepped back and watched her struggle, a numbness invading his whole body.

When she had freed herself she carefully spread the tablecloth on the floor and crawled from corner to corner folding it. Her hair was disarrayed and she couldn't catch her breath.

He followed each of her movements with intense dual concentration. He folded it ten times in his mind before she kneeled in triumph beside the immaculate white rectangle.

11

The house had been built at the beginning of the century. There were still some coloured panes in the window. The city had installed modern fluorescent street-lamps on Stanley, which cast a ghostly yellow light. Shining through the blue and green Victorian glass the result was intense artificial moonlight and the flesh of any woman looked fresh and out-of-doors.

His guitar was always handy. The cedar wood was cool against his stomach. The inside of the guitar smelled like the cigar boxes his father used to have. The tone was excellent in the middle of the night. In those late hours the purity of the music surprised and almost convinced him that he was

creating a sacramental relationship with the girl, the outside
city, and himself.

Breavman and Tamara were cruel to each other. They used
infidelity as a weapon for pain and an incentive for passion.
And they kept returning to the bed on Stanley Street and the
strange light which seemed to repair the innocence of their
bodies. There they would lie for hours, unable to touch or
speak. Sometimes he would be able to comfort her and sometimes she him. They used their bodies but that became more
and more difficult. They were living off each other, had tubes
to each other's guts. The reasons were too deep and original
for him to discover.

He remembers terrible silences and crying he couldn't
come close to. There was nothing he could do, least of all get
dressed and leave. He hated himself for hurting her and he
hated her for smothering him.

He should have kept running that bright morning.

She made him helpless. They made each other helpless.

Breavman let Tamara see some notes of a long story he was
writing. The characters in it were named Tamara and
Lawrence and it took place in a room.

"How ardent you are!" Tamara said theatrically. "Tonight
you are my ardent lover. Tonight we are gentry and animals,
birds and lizards, slime and marble. Tonight we are glorious and
degraded, knighted and crushed, beautiful and disgusting.
Sweat is perfume. Gasps are bells. I wouldn't trade this for the
ravages of the loveliest swan. This is why I must have come to you
in the first place. This is why I must have left the others, the hundreds who tried to stay my ankle with crippled hands as I sped to
you."

"Horseshit," I said.

She eased herself out of my arms' clasp and stood on the
bed. I thought of the thighs of stone colossi but I didn't say
anything.

She stretched out her arms shoulder high.

"Christ of the Andes," she proclaimed.

I kneeled below her and nuzzled her delta.

"Heal me, heal me." I mimicked a prayer.

"Heal me yourself." She laughed and collapsed over me, her face finally resting on my belly.

When we were quiet I said, "Woman, thou art loosed from thine infirmity."

She swung her legs on to the floor, danced over to the table and lit the candle in my tin Mexican candelabra. Holding the light over her head like a religious banner she danced back to the bedside and took my hand.

"Come with me, my beast, my swan," she canted. "The mirror, eunuchs, the mirror!"

We stood before the mirror.

"Who shall say we are not beautiful?" she challenged.

"Yeah."

For a minute or two we inspected our bodies. She put the candelabra down. We embraced.

"Life has not passed us by," she said with imitation nostalgia. "Ah. Alas. Sorrow. Moon. Love."

I tried to be funny. I hoped that our sentimental hoaxing would not lead her to reflect in earnest. That was a process I couldn't take.

I sat on a chair in front of the window and she sat on my lap.

"We are lovers," she began, as if she were stating geometry axioms before attempting the proposition. "If one of those people down there were to look up, someone with very good eyes, he would see a naked woman held by a naked man. That person would be immediately aroused, wouldn't he? The way we become aroused when we read a provoking sexual description in a novel."

I winced at the word sexual. There is no word more inappropriate to lovers.

"And that is the way," she went on, "most lovers try to look

at one another, even after they have been intimate for a long time."

Intimate. That was another of those words.

"It's a great mistake," she said. "The thrill of the forbidden, the thrill of the naughty is quickly expended and lovers are soon bored with one another. Their sexual identities become more and more vague until they are lost altogether."

"What's the alternative?" She was beginning to get me.

"It's to make that which is permitted, thrilling. The lover must totally familiarize himself with his beloved. He must know her every movement: the motion of her buttocks when she walks, the direction of every tiny earthquake when she heaves her chest, the way her thighs spread like lava when she sits down. He must know the sudden coil her stomach makes just before the brink of climax, each orchard of hair, blonde and black, the path of pores on the nose, the chart of vessels in her eyes. He must know her so completely that she becomes, in effect, his own creation. He has moulded the shape of her limbs, distilled her smell. This is the only successful kind of sexual love: the love of the creator for his creation. In other words, the love of the creator for himself. This love can never change."

Her voice became more and more charged as she spoke. She delivered the last words in a kind of frenzy. I had ceased to caress her. Her clinical terms nearly sickened me.

"What is the matter?" she said. "Why have you stopped holding me?"

"Why must you always do this? I've just made love to you. Isn't that enough? Do you have to begin an operation, an autopsy? Sexual, intimate, distil – Jesus Christ! I don't want to memorize everything. I want to be surprised every once in a while. Where are you going?"

She stood before me. The candlelight sketched her mouth hardened with anger.

"Surprised! You're a fool. Like a dozen other men I've had

'ho wanted to make love in the dark, in silence, eyes bound, ears
uffed. Men who tired of me and I of them. And you fly off
cause I want something different for us. You don't know the
fference between creation and masturbation. And there is a
fference. You didn't understand a thing I said."

"Double-talk," I shouted, "double-talk, touble-dock."

I spluttered and covered my face. How had I come to be in this
om?

"We don't know what we're saying," she said, the anger gone.
"Why couldn't you just lie in my arms?"

"Oh, you're hopeless!" she snapped. "Where are my things?"

I watched her dress, my mind a blank, numb. She dressed,
vering her flesh one area after the other, and the numbness
ew and got my throat like a wind of ether. It seemed to dissolve
y skin and blur me with the air of the room.

She walked to the door. I waited for the noise of the latch. She
used, her hand on the knob.

"Stay. Please."

She ran to me and we hugged. The texture of her clothes felt
nny against my skin. She wet my neck and cheek with tears.

"We haven't the time to hurt each other," she whispered.

"Don't cry."

"We can't tire of one another."

During her grief I got hold of myself again. I've noted many
mes during my life that only when faced with extremes of emo-
on in others can I confirm my own stability. Her grief restored
e, made me manly and compassionate.

I led her to the bed.

"You are beautiful," I said. "You always will be."

Soon she fell asleep in my arms. Her body was heavier than it
ad been. She seemed laden and swollen with sorrow. I dreamed
a huge cloak thrown on my shoulders from a weeping man in a
ving cart.

In the morning she had left, as usual, before I awakened.

Tamara read it carefully.

"But I don't talk that way," she said softly.

"Neither do I," said Breavman.

The act of writing had been completed when he handed her the manuscript. He no longer felt ownership.

"But you do, Larry. You talk like both characters."

"All right, I talk like both characters."

"Please don't get angry. I'm trying to understand why you wrote it."

They were lying in the eternal room on Stanley Street. The fluorescent lights across the street provided moonlight.

"I don't care why I wrote it. I just wrote it, that's all."

"And gave it to me."

"Yes."

"Why? You knew it would hurt me."

"You're supposed to be interested in my work."

"Oh, Larry, you know that I am."

"Well, that's why I gave it to you."

"We don't seem to be able to talk."

"What do you want me to say?"

"Nothing."

The silence began. The bed became like a prison surrounded by electric wires. He couldn't get off it or even move. He was gnawed by the notion that this was where he belonged, right on this bed, bandaged with silence. It was what he deserved, all he was fit for.

He told himself that he should just open his mouth and speak. Simple. Just say words. Break up the silence with a remark. Talk about the story. If only he could assault the silence. Then they could make warm and friendly love and talk like strangers right up to morning.

"Was it to tell me that you want to end it between us?"

She's made a brave attempt. Now I must try to answer her. I'll tell her I wanted to challenge her love with a display venom. She'll say, Oh that's what I wanted to hear, and she'll hug me to prove that the venom failed.

All I have to do is force open my teeth, operate the hinges of my jaw, vibrate vocal chords. One word will do it. One word will wedge into the silence and split it open.

"Just try to say something, Larry. I know it's hard."

Any noise, Breavman, any noise, any noise, any noise.

Using his brain like a derrick, he lifted his twenty-ton hand and lowered it on her breast. He sent his fingers through buttonholes. Her skin made the tips of his fingers warm. He loved her for being warm.

"Oh, come here," she said.

They undressed as if they were being chased. He tried to make up for his silence with his tongue and teeth. She had to put his face gently away from her nipple. He praised her loins with a conversation of moans.

"Please say something this time."

He knew if he touched her face he would feel tears. He lay still. He didn't think he ever wanted to move again. He was ready to stay that way for days, catatonic.

She moved to touch him and her motion released him like a spring. This time she didn't stop him. She resigned herself to his numbness. He said everything he could with his body.

They lay quietly.

"Do you feel OK?" he said, and suddenly he was talking his head off.

He rehearsed all his plans for obscure glory and they laughed. He told her poems and they decided he was going to be great. She pitied him for his courage as he described the demons on his shoulders.

"Get away, you dirty old things." She kissed his neck.

"Some on my stomach, too."

After a while Tamara fell asleep. That was what he had been talking against. Her sleeping seemed like a desertion. It always happened when he felt most awake. He was ready to make immortal declarations.

Her hand rested on his arm like snow on a leaf, ready to slip off when he moved.

He lay beside her, an insomniac with visions of vastness. He thought of desert stretches so huge no Chosen People could cross them. He counted grains of sand like sheep and he knew his job would last forever. He thought of aeroplane views of wheatlands so high he couldn't see which way the wind was bending the stalks. Arctic territories and sled-track distances.

Miles he would never cover because he could never abandon this bed.

12

Still Breavman and Krantz often used to drive through the whole night. They'd listen to pop tunes on the local stations or classics from the United States. They'd head north to the Laurentians or east to the Townships.

Breavman imagined the car they were in as seen from above. A small black pellet hurtling across the face of the earth. Free as a meteor and maybe as doomed.

They fled past fields of blue snow. The icy crust kept a stroke of moonlight the way rippled water does. The heater was going full blast. They had nowhere to be in the morning, only lectures and that didn't count. Everything above the snow was black – trees, shacks, whole villages.

Moving at that speed they were not bound to anything. They could sample all the possibilities. They flashed by trees that took a hundred years to grow. They tore through towns where men lived their whole lives. They knew the land was old, the mountains the most ancient on earth. They covered it all at eighty miles an hour.

There was something disdainful in their speed, disdainful

of the eons it took the mountains to smooth out, of the generations of muscle which had cleared the fields, of the labour which had gone into the modern road they rolled on. They were aware of the disdain. The barbarians must have ridden Roman highways with the same feeling. We have the power now. Who cares what went before?

And there was something frightened in their speed. Back in the city their families were growing like vines. Mistresses were teaching a sadness no longer lyrical but claustrophobic. The adult community was insisting that they choose an ugly particular from the range of beautiful generalities. They were flying from their majority, from the real bar mitzvah, the real initiation, the real and vicious circumcision which society was hovering to inflict through limits and dull routine.

They spoke gently to the French girls in the diners where they stopped. They were so pathetic, false-toothed and frail. They'd forget them in the next twenty miles. What were they doing behind the Arborite counters? Dreaming of Montreal neon?

The highway was empty. They were the only two in flight and that knowledge made them deeper friends than ever. It elated Breavman. He'd say, "Krantz, all they'll ever find of us is a streak of oil on the garage floor without even rainbows in it." Lately Krantz had been very silent, but Breavman was certain he was thinking the same things. Everyone they knew or who loved them was sleeping miles behind the exhaust. If the radio music was rock-and-roll, they understood the longing of it; if it was Handel, they understood the majesty.

At some point in these rides Breavman would proposition himself like this: Breavman, you're eligible for many diverse experiences in this best of all possible worlds. There are many beautiful poems which you will write and be praised for, many desolate days when you won't be able to lay pen to paper. There will be many lovely cunts to lie in, different colours of skin to kiss, various orgasms to encounter, and many nights you will walk out your lust, bitter and alone. There will be many heights of emotion, intense sunsets, exalting insights, creative pain, and many murderous plateaux of indifference where you won't even own your personal despair. There will be many good hands of power you can play with ruthlessness or benevolence, many vast skies to lie under and congratulate yourself on humility, many galley rides of suffocating slavery. This is what waits for you. Now, Breavman, here is the proposition. Let us suppose that you could spend the rest of your life exactly as you are at this very minute, in this car hurtling towards brush country, at this precise stop on the road beside a row of white guide posts, always going past these posts at eighty, this juke-box song of rejection pumping, this particular sky of clouds and stars, your mind including this immediate cross-section of memory – which would you choose? Fifty more years of this car ride, or fifty more of achievement and failure?

And Breavman never hesitated in his choice.

Let it go on as it is right now. Let the speed never diminish. Let the snow remain. Let me never be removed from this partnership with my friend. Let us never find different things to do. Let us never evaluate one another. Let the moon stay on one side of the road. Let the girls be a gold blur in my mind, like the haze of the moon, or the neon glow above the city. Let the compounded electric guitar keep throbbing under the declaration:

> *When I lost my baby*
> *I almost lost my mind.*

Let the edges of the hills be just about to brighten. Let the trees never fuzz with leaves. Let the black towns sleep in one long night like Lesbia's lover. Let the monks in the half-built monasteries remain on their knees in the 4 A.M. Latin prayer. Let Pat Boone stand on the highest rung of the Hit Parade and tell all the factory night shifts:

I went to see the gypsy
To have my fortune read.

Let snow always dignify the auto graveyards on the road to Ayer's Cliff. Let the nailed shacks of apple vendors never show polished apples and hints of cider.

But let me remember what I remember of orchards. Let me keep my tenth of a second's worth of fantasy and recollection, showing all the layers like a geologist's sample. Let the Caddie or the VW run like a charm, let it go like a bomb, let it blast. Let the tune make the commercial wait forever.

I can tell you, people,
The news was not so good.

The news is great. The news is sad but it's in a song so it's not so bad. Pat is doing all my poems for me. He's got lines to a million people. It's all I wanted to say. He's distilled the sorrow, glorified it in an echo chamber. I don't need my typewriter. It's not the piece of luggage I suddenly remembered I forgot. No pencils, ball-pens, pad. I don't even want to draw in the mist on the windshield. I can make up sagas in my head all the way to Baffin Island but I don't have to write them down. Pat, you've snitched my job, but you're such a good guy, old-time American success, naïve big winner, that it's okay. The PR men have convinced me that you are a humble kid. I can't resent you. My only criticism is: be more desperate, try and sound more agonized or we'll have to get a Negro to replace you:

She said my baby's left me
And she's gone for good.

Don't let the guitars slow down like locomotive wheels. Don't let the man at CKVL tell me what I've just been listening to. Sweet sounds, reject me not. Let the words go on like the landscape we're never driving out of.

gone for good

OK, let the last syllable endure. This is the tenth of a second I've traded all the presidencies for. The telephone poles are playing intricate games of Cat's Cradle with the rushing wires. The snow is piled like the Red Sea on either side of our fenders. We're not expected and we're not missed. We put all our money in the gas tank, we're fat as camels in the Sahara. The hurtling car, the trees, the moon and its light on the fields of snow, the resigned grinding chords of the tune – everything is poised in perfection for the quick freeze, the eternal case in the astral museum.

   good

So long, mister, mistress, rabbi, doctor. 'Bye. Don't forget your salesman's bag of adventure samples. My friend and I, we'll stay right here – on our side of the speed limit. Won't we, Krantz, won't we, Krantz, won't we, Krantz?

   "Want to stop for a hamburger?" says Krantz as though he were musing on an abstract theory.

   "Now or one of these days?"

13

Breavman and Tamara were white. Everybody else on the beach had a long summer tan. Krantz was positively bronze.

   "I feel extra naked," said Tamara, "as if I had taken off a layer of skin with my clothes. I wish they'd take off theirs."

   They relaxed on the hot sand while Krantz supervised the General Swim. He sat on a white-painted wooden tower, megaphone in one hand, whistle in the other.

   The water was silver with thrashing bodies. His whistle pierced the cries and laughter and suddenly the waterfront was silent. At his command the campers paired off, lifting their joined hands out of the water at their turns.

   Then, in succession, the counsellors posted along the

docks snapped, "Check!" A hundred and fifty children kept still. The safety check over, Krantz blew his whistle again and the general din was resumed.

Krantz in the role of disciplinarian surprised Breavman. He knew Krantz had worked many summers at a children's camp, but he always thought of him (now that he examined it) as one of the children, or let's say, the best child, devising grand nocturnal tricks, first figure of a follow-the-leader game through the woods.

But here he was, master of the beach, bronze and squint-eyed, absolute. Children and water obeyed him. Stopping and starting the noise and laughter and splashing with the whistle blast, Krantz seemed to be cutting into the natural progression of time like a movie frozen into a single image and then released to run again. Breavman had never suspected him of that command.

Breavman and Tamara were city-white, and it separated them from the brown bodies as if they were second-rate harmless lepers.

Breavman was surprised to discover on Tamara's thigh a squall of tiny gold hairs. Her black hair was loose and the intense sun picked out metallic highlights.

It wasn't just that they were white – they were white together, and their whiteness seemed to advertise some daily unclean indoor ritual which they shared.

"When the Negroes take over," Breavman said, "this is the way we're going to feel all the time."

"But isn't Krantz marvellous?"

They both stared at him, as if for the first time.

Perhaps it was this curious fracturing of time of Krantz's whistle that removed Breavman into the slow-motion movie which was always running somewhere in his mind.

He is watching himself from a long way off. The whistle has silenced the water-play. Even the swallows seem motionless, poised, pinned at the top of ladders of air.

This part of the film is overexposed. It hurts his eyes to remember but he loves to stare.

Overexposed and double-exposed. The Laurentian summer sun is behind every image, turning one to silhouette, another to shining jelly transparency.

The diver is Krantz. Here he is folded in a jackknife in the air above the water, half silver, half black. The splash rises slowly around the disappearing feet like feathers out of a black crater.

A cheer goes up from the children as he climbs up on the dock. All his movements have an intensity, the smallest gesture a quality of power, close-up size. The children surround him and try to touch his wet shoulders.

"But isn't Krantz marvellous?"

Now Krantz is running toward his friends, sand sticking to his soles. He is smiling a welcome.

Now Tamara is not touching Breavman, she had been lying close to him, but now nothing of her is touching.

She stands automatically and Krantz's eyes and her eyes, they invade the screen and change from welcome to surprise to question to desire – here the picture is stopped dead and pockmarked by suns – and now they annihilate all the bodies on the sand, for an enduring fraction they are rushing only to each other.

The swallows fall naturally and the ordinary chaos returns as Krantz laughs.

"It's about time you people paid me a visit."

The three of them hugged and talked wildly.

14

Tamara and Breavman graduated from college. There was no longer any framework around their battered union, so down it came. They were lucky the parting was not bitter. They were both fed up with pain. Each had slept with about a dozen people and they had used every name as a weapon. It was a torture-list of friends and enemies.

They parted over a table in a coffee-shop. You could get wine in teacups if you knew the proprietress and asked in French.

All along he had known that he never knew her and never would. Adoration of thighs is not enough. He never cared who Tamara was, only what she represented. He confessed this to her and they talked for three hours.

"I'm sorry, Tamara. I want to touch people like a magician, to change them or hurt them, leave my brand, make them beautiful. I want to be the hypnotist who takes no chances of falling asleep himself. I want to kiss with one eye open. Or I did. I don't want to any more."

She loved the way he talked.

They returned to the room on Stanley, unofficially, from time to time. A twenty-year-old can be very tender to an ancient mistress.

"I know I never saw you. I blur everyone in my personal vision. I never get their own music. . . ."

After a while her psychiatrist thought it would be better if she didn't see him again.

15

Breavman won a scholarship to do graduate work in English at Columbia but he decided not to take it.

"Oh no, Krantz, nothing smells more like a slaughterhouse than a graduate seminar. People sitting around tables in small classrooms, their hands bloody with commas. They get older and the ages of the poets remain the same, twenty-three, twenty-five, nineteen."

"That gives you four years at the outside, Breavman."

His book of Montreal sketches appeared and was well

received. He started seeing it on the bookshelves of his friends and relatives and he resented their having it. It was none of their business how Tamara's breasts looked in the artificial moonlight of Stanley Street.

Canadians are desperate for a Keats. Literary meetings are the manner in which Anglophiles express passion. He read his sketches for small societies, large college groups, enlightened church meetings. He slept with as many pretty chairwomen as he could. He gave up conversation. He merely quoted himself. He could maintain an oppressive silence at a dinner-table to make the lovely daughter of the house believe he was brooding over her soul.

The only person he could joke with was Krantz.

The world was being hoaxed by a disciplined melancholy. All the sketches made a virtue of longing. All that was necessary to be loved widely was to publish one's anxieties. The whole enterprise of art was a calculated display of suffering.

He walked with pale blonde girls along Westmount Boulevard. He told them he saw the stone houses as ruins. He hinted that they could fulfil themselves through him. He could lean against a fireplace with all the ambiguous tragedy of a blind Samson against the temple pillars.

Among certain commercial Jews he was considered a mild traitor who could not be condemned outright. They were dismayed by the possibility that he might make a financial success out of what he was doing. This their ulcers resented. His name was in the newspapers. He might not be an ideal member of the community but neither was Disraeli or Mendelssohn, whose apostasies the Jewish regard for attainment has always overlooked. Also, writing is an essential part of the Jewish tradition and even the degraded contemporary situation cannot suppress it. A respect for books and artistry will persist for another generation or two. It can't go on forever without being reconsecrated.

Among certain Gentiles he was suspect for other reasons.

His Semitic barbarity hidden under the cloak of Art, he was intruding on their cocktail rituals. They were pledged to Culture (like all good Canadians) but he was threatening the blood purity of their daughters. They made him feel as vital as a Negro. He engaged stockbrokers in long conversations about over-breeding and the loss of creative vitality. He punctuated his speech with Yiddish expressions which he never thought of using anywhere else. In their living-rooms, for no reason at all, he often broke into little Hasidic dances around the tea table.

He incorporated Sherbrooke Street into his general domain. He believed he understood its elegant sadness better than anyone else in the city. Whenever he went into one of the stores he always remembered that he was standing in what was once the drawing-room of a smart town house. He breathed a historical sigh for the mansions become brewery and insurance head offices. He sat on the steps of the museum and watched the chic women float into dress shops or walk their rich dogs in front of the Ritz. He watched people line up for buses, board, and zoom away. He always found that a mystery. He walked into lavatory-like new banks and wondered what everyone was doing there. He stared at pediments of carved grapevines. Gargoyles on the brown stone church. Intricate wooden balconies just east of Park. The rose window of another church spiked to prevent pigeons from roosting. All the old iron, glass, rock.

He had no plans for the future.

Early one morning he and Krantz (they hadn't gone to bed the night before) sat on a low stone wall at the corner of Mackay and Sherbrooke and admonished the eight-thirty working-day crowds.

"The jig is up," Breavman shouted. "It's all over. Go back to your homes. Do not pass Go. Do not collect two hundred dollars. Go straight to your homes. Return to bed. Can't you see it's all done with?"

"*Consummatum est,*" Krantz said.

Later Breavman said, "You don't really believe it, do you, Krantz?"

"Not as thoroughly as you."

No plans for the future.

He could lay his hand on a low-cut gown and nobody minded. He was a kind of mild Dylan Thomas, talent and behaviour modified for Canadian tastes.

He felt as though he had masturbated on television. He was bereft of privacy, restraint, discretion.

"Do you know what I am, Krantz?"

"Yes, and don't recite the catalogue."

"A stud for unhappy women. A twilight peeper of Victorian ruins. A middle-class connoisseur of doomed union songs. A race-haunted exhibitionist forever waving my circumcision. A lap-dog who laps."

Therefore, according to the traditions of his class, he did penance through manual labour.

On one of his walks around the Montreal waterfront he passed a brass foundry, a small firm which manufactured bathroom fixtures. A window was open and he looked inside.

The air was smoke-filled. Loud incessant noise of machinery. Against the wall were hills of mud-coloured sand. At the far end of the foundry stone crucibles glowed in sunken furnaces. The men were covered with grime. They heaved heavy sand moulds. Through the smoke they looked like figures in one of those old engravings of Purgatorio.

Then a red-hot crucible was raised out of the furnace by a pulley system and swung towards the row of moulds. It was lowered to the ground and the slag scooped off the surface.

Now a huge man wearing an asbestos apron and goggles took over. He guided the crucible over to the moulds. With a lever device he tilted the stone pot and poured the molten brass into the lead-holes of the moulds.

Breavman gasped at the brightness of the liquid metal. It

was the colour gold should be. It was as beautiful as flesh. It was the colour of gold he thought of when he read the word in prayers or poems. It was yellow, alive and screaming. It poured out in an arch with smoke and white sparks. He watched the man move up and down the rows, dispensing this glory. He looked like a monolithic idol. No, he was a true priest.

That was the job he wanted but that wasn't what he got. He became a core-wire puller. Unskilled. Pay was seventy-five cents an hour. The hours were seven-thirty to five-thirty, half-hour for lunch.

The size of the core determines the size of the hole running through the faucets. It is made of baked sand packed along a length of wire. It is placed between the two halves of the mould, and the brass flows around it, creating the hole. When the moulds are broken up and the rough-cast faucets extracted they still contain the wire on which the cores were suspended.

His job was to pull these wires out. He sat on a box not far from the long, low roller tables on which the moulds were placed for filling. Beside him was a heap of hot faucets with these core-wires sticking out from the ends. He seized one with his left gloved hand and yanked out the twisted wire with a pair of pliers.

He pulled several thousand wires a week. The only time he stopped was to watch the pouring of the brass. It turned out that the moulder was a Negro. It was impossible to tell with the grime on everybody's face. Now there's a heroic proletarian tale if he ever heard one.

Pull your wire, Breavman.

The beauty of the brass never diminished.

He took his place in the fire and smoke and sand. The foundry was not air-conditioned, thank heaven. His hands grew callouses which were ordinary to working girls but they were stroked like medals by others.

He sat on his box and looked around. He had come to the right place. Chopping machines and the roar of furnaces were exactly the right music to purge. Sweat and mud on a man's pimpled back was a picture to give perspective to flesh. The air was foul: the intake of breath after a nostalgic sigh coated your throat with scum. The view of old men and young men condemned to their sandpiles added an excellent dimension to his vision of lambs, beasts, and little children. The roof windows let in shafts of dirty sunlight which were eventually lost in the general fumes. They laboured in a gloom tinted red by the fires. He had become an integrated figure in the inferno engraving which he had glimpsed a few weeks before.

The firm was not unionized. He thought about contacting the appropriate union and helping to organize the place. But that wasn't why he had come. He'd come for boredom and penance. He introduced an Irish immigrant to Walt Whitman and talked him into going to a night school. That was the extent of his social work.

The boredom was killing. Manual labour did not free his mind to wander at will. It numbed his mind, but the anaesthesia was not sufficiently potent to deliver it from awareness. It could still recognize its bondage. He would suddenly realize that he had been chanting the same tune over and over for the last hour. Each wire represented a small crisis and each extraction a small triumph. He could not overlook this absurdity.

The more bored he became the more inhuman was the beauty of the brass. It was too bright to look at. You needed goggles. It was too hot to stand close to. You needed an apron. Many times a day he watched the metal being poured, feeling the heat even where he sat. The arch of liquid came to represent an intensity he would never achieve.

He punched the clock every morning for a year.

16

His friend was leaving Montreal to study in England.

"But, Krantz, it's Montreal you're leaving, Montreal on the very threshold of greatness, like Athens, like New Orleans."

"The Frogs are vicious," he said, "the Jews are vicious, the English are absurd."

"That's why we're great, Krantz. The cross-fertilization."

"Okay, Breavman, you stay here to chronicle the Renaissance."

It was an early summer evening on Stanley Street. Breavman had been in the foundry for a month. The strolling girls had their bare arms on.

"Krantz, the arms, the bosoms, the buttocks, O lovely catalogue!"

"They've certainly come out."

"Krantz, do you know why Sherbrooke Street is so bloody beautiful?"

"Because you want to get laid."

Breavman thought for a second.

"You're right, Krantz."

It was great to be back in the dialogue with Krantz; he hadn't seen him very much in the past few weeks.

But he knew the street was beautiful for other reasons. Because you've stores and people living in the same buildings. When you've got only stores, especially modern-fronted ones, there is a terrible stink of cold money-grabbing. When you've got only houses, or rather when the houses get too far from the stores, they exude some poisonous secret, like a plantation or an abattoir.

But what Krantz said was true. No, not laid. Beauty at close quarters.

A half-block up, a girl turned down to Sherbrooke. She was strolling alone.

"Remember, Krantz, three years ago we would have followed her with all kinds of fleshly dreams."

"And fled if she ever looked back."

The girl ahead of them walked under a lamplight, the light sliding down the folds of her hair. Breavman began to whistle "Lili Marlene."

"Krantz, we're walking into a European movie. You and me are old officers walking along to something important. Sherbrooke is a ruin. Why does it feel like a war just ended?"

"Because you want to get laid."

"C'mon, Krantz, give me a chance."

"Breavman, if I gave you a chance, you'd weep through every summer night."

"Do you know what I'm going to do, Krantz? I'm going to walk up to that girl and be very gentle and polite and ask her to join us for a small walk over the world."

"You do that, Breavman."

He quickened his pace and moved beside her. This would be it. All the compassion of strangers. She turned her face and looked at him.

"Excuse me," he said and stopped. "Mistake."

She walked away and he waited for Krantz to catch up.

"She was a beast, Krantz. We couldn't have toasted her. She wasn't all that is beautiful in women."

"It's not our night."

"There's lots of night left."

"I've got to get up early for the boat."

But they did not go right back to Stanley. They walked slowly up the streets towards home: University, Metcalfe, Peel, MacTavish. Named for the distinguished from the British Isles. They passed by the stone houses and the black iron fences. Many of the houses had been taken over by the university or turned into boarding-houses, but here and there colonel or a lady still lived, manicured the lawns and bushes, still climbed the stone steps as if all the neighbours were peers. They wandered through the campus of the university. Night, like time, gave all the buildings a deep dignity. There was the library with its crushing cargo of words, dark and stone.

"Krantz, let's get out of here. The buildings are starting to claim me."

"I know what you mean, Breavman."

As they walked back to Stanley, Breavman was no longer in a movie. All he wanted to do was turn to Krantz and wish him luck, all the luck in the world. There was nothing else to say to a person.

The taxis were beginning to pile up in front of the tourist houses. Half a block down you could get whisky in coffee cups at a blind pig disguised as a bridge club. They watched the taximen making U-turns in the one-way street: friends of the police. They knew all the landladies and store owners and waitresses. They were citizens of downtown. And Krantz was taking off like a big bird.

"You know, Breavman, you're not Montreal's suffering servant."

"Of course I am. Can't you see me, crucified on a maple tree at the top of Mount Royal? The miracles are just beginning to happen. I have just enough breath to tell them, 'I told you so, you cruel bastards.'"

"Breavman, you're a schmuck."

And soon their dialogue would be broken. They stood on the balcony in silence, watching the night-doings get into gear.

"Krantz, do I have anything to do with you leaving?"

"A little."

"I'm sorry."

"We've got to stop interpreting the world for one another."

"Yes . . . yes."

The buildings were so familiar and the street so well known. Even Gautama wept when he lost a friend. Nothing

would be the same tomorrow. He could hardly bear to understand that. Krantz wouldn't be there. That would be like a
bulldozer turned loose in the heart of the city. They weren't
the kind of people that wrote letters to each other.

Krantz took a long glance around him. "Yup," he said, like
an old farmer in a rocking chair.

"Yup," Breavman agreed over nothing.

"Just about time," said Krantz.

"Good night, Krantz."

"Good night, old Breavman."

He smiled and clasped his friend's hand.

"Good night, old Krantz," and they joined four hands and
then went into their separate rooms.

17

Montreal was madly buying records of Leadbelly and the
Weavers and rushing down to Gesu Hall in mink coats to hear
Pete Seeger sing socialist songs. Breavman was at the party by
virtue of his reputation as a folk singer and minor celebrity.
The hostess had subtly suggested on the phone that he bring
his guitar, but he didn't. He hadn't touched it for months.

"Larry! It's so good to see you; it's been years!"

"You look beautiful, Lisa."

With his first glance of appreciation he claimed her,
because of the street they had lived on, because he knew the
whiteness of her, because her skipping body was bound to his
by red string. She lowered her eyes.

"Thank you, Larry. And you've managed to become
famous."

"Hardly famous, but it's a good word."

"We saw you interviewed on TV last week."

"In this country writers are interviewed on TV for one reason only: to give the rest of the nation a good laugh."

"Everybody says you're very clever."

"Everybody is a vicious gossip."

He brought her a drink and they talked. She told him about her children, two boys, and they exchanged information about their families. Her husband was on a business trip. He and her father were opening automatic bowling alleys right across the country. Knowing she was alone launched Breavman's fantasies. Of course she was alone, of course he had met her that specific night, she would be delivered to him.

"Lisa, now that you have children, do you ever think about your own childhood?"

"I always used to promise myself that when I grew up I'd remember exactly how it was, and treat my children from that viewpoint."

"And do you?"

"It's very hard. You'd be surprised how much you forget and how little time there is to remember. Usually you act right on the spot and hope your decision is the best one."

"Do you remember Bertha?" was the first of the questions he meant to ask.

"Yes, but didn't she –"

"Do you remember me?"

"Of course."

"What was I like?"

"I suppose you'd be annoyed if I said you were like any other ten-year-old boy. I don't know, Larry. You were a nice boy."

"Do you remember the Soldier and the Whore?"

"What?"

"Do you remember my green pants?"

"You're getting silly. . . ."

"I wish you remembered everything."

"Why? If we remembered everything we'd never be able to do anything."

"If you remembered what I remember you'd be in bed with me right now," he said blindly.

Lisa was kind, wise, or interested enough not to make a joke of what he said.

"No, I wouldn't. Even if I wanted to, I wouldn't. I'm too selfish or scared or prudish, or whatever it is, to risk what I've got. I want to keep everything I have."

"So do I. I don't want to forget anyone I was ever connected with."

"You don't have to. Especially me. I'm glad I met you tonight. You have to come over and meet Carl and the children. Carl reads a lot, I'm sure you'd enjoy talking to him."

"The last thing I intend to do is talk books with anybody, even Carl. I want to sleep with you. It's very simple."

He had intended by his recklessness to reach her quickly and disarm her, but he succeeded only in making the conversation fashionable.

"It's not simple for me. I'm not trying to be funny. Why do you want to sleep with me?"

"Because we once held hands."

"And that's a reason?"

"Humans are lucky to be connected in any way at all, even by the table between them."

"But you can't be connected to everyone. It wouldn't mean anything then."

"It would to me."

"But is going to bed the only way a man and woman can be connected?"

Breavman replied in terms of the flirtation, not out of his real experience.

"What else is there? Conversation? I'm in the business and I have no faith in words whatever. Friendship? A friendship between a man and a woman which is not based on sex is either hypocrisy or masochism. When I see a woman's face transformed by the orgasm we have reached together, then I know we've met. Anything else is fiction. That's the vocabulary we speak in today. It's the only language left."

"Then it's a language which nobody understands. It's just become a babble."

"Better than silence. Lisa, let's get out of here. Any moment now someone's going to ask why I didn't bring my guitar, and I'm liable to smash him in the mouth. Let's talk over coffee, somewhere."

She shook her head gently. "No."

It was the best no he ever heard because it had in it dignity, appreciation, and firm denial. It claimed him and ended the game. He was content now to talk, watch her, and wonder just as he had when the young men in white scarves had taken her away in their long cars.

"I've never heard that word spoken better."

"I thought it was what you wanted to hear."

"How did you get so damn wise?"

"Look out, Larry."

"Look what we found." The hostess beamed. Several guests had followed her over.

"I've never heard you play," Lisa said. "I'd like to."

He took the unfamiliar guitar and tuned it. The record-player was turned off and everyone drew chairs around or sat on the thick carpet.

It was a good Spanish instrument, very light wood, resonant bass strings. He hadn't held a guitar for months but as soon as he struck the first chord (*A* minor) he was happy he'd agreed to play.

The first chord is always crucial for him. Sometimes it sounds tinny, bland, and the best thing he can do is put the instrument away, because the tone never improves and all his inventions jingle like commercials. This happens when he approaches the instrument without the proper respect or affection. It rebukes him like a complying frigid woman.

But there are those good times when the tone is deep and lingering, and he cannot believe it is himself who is strumming the strings. He watches the intricate blur of his right hand and the ballet-fingers of his left hand stepping between the frets, and he wonders what connection there is between all that movement and the music in the air, which seems to come from the wood itself.

It was like that when he played and sang only for Lisa. He sang the Spanish Civil War songs, not as a partisan, but as a Tiresian historian. He sang the minor songs of absence, thinking of Donne's beautiful opening,

> *Sweetest love! I do not go*
> *For weariness of thee,*

which is the essence of any love song. He hardly sang the words, he spoke them. He rediscovered the poetry which had overwhelmed him years before, the easy line that gave itself carelessly away and then, before it was over, struck home.

> *I'd rather be in some dark valley*
> *Where the sun don't never shine,*
> *Than to see my true love love another*
> *When I know that she should be mine.*

He played for an hour, aiming all the melody at Lisa. While he sang he wanted to untie the red string and let her free. That was the best gift he could give her.

When it was over and he had put the guitar away carefully, as though it contained the finer part of him, Lisa said, "That made me feel more connected to you than anything you said. Please come to our house soon."

"Thank you."

Soon he slipped out of the party for a walk on the mountain. He watched the moon and it didn't move for a long time.

18

Four days later the phone rang at one-thirty in the morning. Breavman bolted for it, happy to break his working schedule. He knew everything she was going to say.

"I didn't think you'd be asleep," Lisa said.

"I'm not. But you should be."

"I'd like to see you."

"I'd like to see you too, but I've got a better idea: put down the telephone and visit each of your children's rooms and then go to bed."

"I did that. Twice."

It was a free country. The old taboos were in disrepute. They were grown up and wouldn't be called in for supper. She was twenty-odd, wealthy, white, with a fast car and an out-of-town husband, classic commercial widow. He was alone with his insomnia and bad manuscripts.

Breavman, thou false lech, your room hideously empty as your charity smile. I knew she'd be delivered, Krantz.

She broke the silence. "Do you want me to come down?"

"Yes."

He jammed all his laundry in the closet and hid an egg-caked plate in a stack of clean ones. He sat at his desk and slowly bound up his manuscript, taking an unfamiliar pleasure in the act, as if he now had some special right to contemn the papers.

She was wearing slacks, her black hair was loose, but freshly combed. She brought a clean Laurentian fragrance into the room.

"You smell like you just descended a ski slope."

He poured her a glass of sherry. In a few minutes he had the whole story. Her husband wasn't on a trans-Canada trip, opening bowling alleys. He was in Toronto living with some woman, an employee of the Canadian Broadcasting Corporation.

"My father has the complete detective report. I didn't want details."

"These things happen," Breavman said, its triteness crushing his last word into a mumble.

Lisa talked and sipped her drink calmly, far from losing the coolness she had carried in. He felt that, along with all her precious things, she had left her emotions at home. She knew that these things happen, she knew that everything happens, and so what?

"He'll come back."

Lisa told him with her eyes that her husband didn't need Breavman's defence.

"And you love him, Lisa, and your children, and your home. That's the most obvious thing about you."

She lowered her eyes and studied the wine glass. He thought she must be remembering the rows of crystal in her own house, comparing the disarray of his room with her own household order. But she had come for revenge, and the more distasteful the conditions, the sweeter. Perhaps she was not lonely, perhaps she was offended.

"I don't feel like discussing Carl here."

"I'm glad you came. You made me feel very good the night of the party, the way you listened. I didn't think I'd ever see you alone again, and I wanted to."

"The strange thing is that I decided you were the only one I could see."

Perhaps she could express her revenge with him because he was secret, not part of her life, but not exactly a stranger – like meeting someone from your own town in a foreign place.

So they could sit together, perhaps he could hold her hand, and talk about the curious way things turn out. They could walk along Sherbrooke arm in arm, the end of the summer was coming. He could offer her his company and friendship as solace. Or they could find the bed immediately; there was no in-between.

Wasn't there only one inevitability, and a weary one at that? He walked to her and kissed her mouth. She stood up and they embraced. They both sensed in that moment the mutual need to annihilate thought and speech. She was tired of the offence. He was tired of wondering why he wanted her body, or any body.

They performed the act of love, as he had many times before, a protest against luck and circumstances. He praised her beauty and the ski slopes that had made her legs so fine.

But he did not sleep with Lisa the child. He did not return to the park where nurses watched the sailor children. He did not build a mysterious garage above her naked form. He made love to a woman. Not Lisa. He knew this as they lay together and talked, finally, about their childhood and city. That contract, interrupted by the Curse, would never be fulfilled. This was a woman with whom he was beginning an affair, perhaps. The child that grew away from him into breasts and long cars and adult cigarettes was not the peaceful woman beside him. That child would evade him and cause him to wonder at her always.

The sun had already risen when she dressed to go.

"Get some rest," she said. "I'll call you tomorrow. You'd better not call the house. Never call the house."

He went to the window to watch her drive away. She rolled down her car window and waved at him, and suddenly they were waving harder and longer than people ever do. She was crying and pressing her palm up at him, back and forth in urgent semaphore, as if to erase out of the morning air, please, all contracts, vows, agreements, old or new. He leaned out of the window and with his signalling hand agreed to let the night go, to let her go free, because he had all he needed of her fixed in an afternoon.

19

Some say that no one ever leaves Montreal, for that city, like Canada itself, is designed to preserve the past, a past that happened somewhere else.

This past is not preserved in the buildings or monuments, which fall easily to profit, but in the minds of her citizens. The clothes they wear, the jobs they perform are only the disguises of fashion. Each man speaks with his father's tongue.

Just as there are no Canadians, there are no Montrealers. Ask a man who he is and he names a race.

So the streets change swiftly, the skyscrapers climb into silhouettes against the St. Lawrence, but it is somehow unreal and no one believes it, because in Montreal there is no present tense, there is only the past claiming victories.

Breavman fled the city.

His mother was phoning him daily. She was alone, did he know what that meant? Her back was sore, her legs were swollen. People asked about her son and she had to tell them he was a factory worker.

Breavman laid the phone on the bed and let her talk. He had no strength or skill to comfort her. He sat beside the receiver, unable to speak or think, aware only of the monotonous rasp of her voice.

"I looked in the mirror today, I didn't recognize myself, wrinkles from aggravation, from nights thinking about my son, do I deserve this, fifteen years with a sick man, a son who doesn't care whether his mother lies like a stone, like a dog, a mother, an only mother should lie like a stone, a prostitute wouldn't stand from her son what I stand, do I have so much, do I eat chocolate all day, have I got diamonds for all that I gave away, fifteen years, did I ever ask anything for myself, two broken legs from Russia, swollen ankles that the doctor was surprised, but my son is too busy to hear the truth, night after night I lie in front of the TV, does anybody care what I do, I was such a happy person, I was a beauty, now I'm ugly, people on the street don't recognize me, I gave my life for what, I was so good to everyone, a mother, once in a lifetime you have a mother, do we live forever, a mother is a fragile thing, your best friend, in the whole world does anyone else care what happens to you, you can fall down on the street and people pass you by, and I lie like a stone, all over the world people are running to see their mothers, but to my son it doesn't matter, he can get another mother, one life we have, everything is a dream, it's luck. . . ."

And when she was through he said, "I hope you're feeling better, Mother," and good-bye.

She was seeing a psychiatrist now. He didn't seem to be helping her. Was she taking the pills he prescribed? Her voice sounded more hysterical.

He fled his mother and his family.

He had thought that his tall uncles in their dark clothes were princes of an élite brotherhood. He had thought the synagogue was their house of purification. He had thought their businesses were realms of feudal benevolence. But he had grown to understand that none of them even pretended to these things. They were proud of their financial and communal success. They liked to be first, to be respected, to sit close to the altar, to be called up to lift the scrolls. They weren't pledged to any other idea. They did not believe their blood was consecrated. Where had he got the notion that they did?

When he saw the rabbi and cantor move in their white robes, the light on the brocaded letters of their prayer shawls; when he stood among his uncles and bowed with them and joined his voice to theirs in the responses; when he followed in the prayer book the catalogue of magnificence —

No, his uncles were not grave enough. They were strict, not grave. They did not seem to realize how fragile the ceremony was. They participated in it blindly, as if it would last forever. They did not seem to realize how important they were, not self-important, but important to the incantation, the altar, the ritual. They were ignorant of the craft of devotion. They were merely devoted. They never thought how close the ceremony was to chaos. Their nobility was insecure because it rested on inheritance and not moment-to-moment creation in the face of annihilation.

In the most solemn or joyous part of the ritual Breavman knew the whole procedure could revert in a second to desolation. The cantor, the rabbi, the chosen laymen stood before the open Ark, cradling the Torah scrolls, which looked like stiff-necked royal children, and returned them one by one to their golden stall. The beautiful melody soared, which proclaimed that the Law was a tree of life and a path of peace. Couldn't they see how it had to be nourished? And all these men who bowed, who performed the customary motions, they were unaware that other men had written the sacred tune, other men had developed the seemingly eternal gestures out of clumsy confusion. They took for granted what was dying in their hands.

But why should he care? He wasn't Isaiah, and the people claimed nothing. He didn't even like the people or the god of their cult. He had no rights in the matter.

He didn't want to blame anyone. Why should he feel that they had bred him to a disappointment? He was bitter because he couldn't inherit the glory they unwittingly advertised. He couldn't be part of their brotherhood but he wanted to be among them. A nostalgia for solidarity. Why was his father's pain involved?

He turned away from the city. He had abused the streets with praise. He had expected too much from certain cast-iron fences, special absurd turrets, staircases to the mountain, early-morning views of bridges on the St. Lawrence. He was tired of the mystery he had tried to impute to public squares and gardens. He was tired of the atmosphere in which he tried to involve Peel Street and boarding-house mansions. The city refused to rest quietly under the gauze of melancholy he had draped over the buildings. It reasserted its indifference.

He stood very still.

New York City. He lived in the tower of World Student House. His window overlooked the Hudson River. He was relieved that it wasn't his city and he didn't have to record its ugly magnificence. He walked on whatever streets he wanted and he didn't have to put their names in stories. New York had already been sung. And by great voices. This freed him to stare and taste at will. Everybody spoke a kind of English, no resentment, he could talk to people everywhere. He wandered in the early-morning markets. He asked the names of the fish, stiff and silver in boxes of ice. He attended more of his seminars.

He saw the most beautiful person and pursued her. Shell.

Book III

HER MIDDLE name was Marshell, after her mother's people, but they called her Shell.

Her ancestors crossed the ocean early enough to insure her mother membership in the DAR. The family produced two undistinguished senators and a number of very good traders. For the past seventy-five years all the males (excepting the utterly stupid) have attended Williams. Shell was the second youngest in a family of four. Her older brother was one of the unfortunates who did not make Williams. To compound his shame he ran off with a Baptist and made his father bitterly happy when he quarrelled with his wife over their children's education.

Shell grew up in a large white house on the outskirts of Hartford, where her maternal great-grandfather had founded a successful bank. There were a stone fountain in the garden, many acres of land, and a stream which her father stocked with trout. After the younger son made a reasonable marriage and moved to Pittsburg, Shell and her sister were bought two horses. A stable was built, a miniature reproduction of the house itself. Her father was fond of building miniatures of his house. Scattered through the trees there were a chicken coop, a rabbit hutch, a doll's house, and a bird roost, all copies of the original one, which (they reminded their weekend guests) was for humans.

The affairs of the house were conducted with much ritual and decorum. Both the mother and father, deep readers of American history and collectors of colonial furniture, took some pride in never having been tempted to visit Europe.

Every spring Shell was in charge of floating cut flowers in the stone fountain. She took the business of being a girl very seriously. She thought her sister was too rough, wondered why her mother raised her voice, was hurt when she contradicted her husband. Not only did she believe in fairy tales, she experimented with peas under her mattress.

She hated her hair, which was black, thick, and long. After a washing it could not be managed and she was called "Zulu." But she would not cut it, thinking perhaps of ladders let down from tower windows. She didn't like her body. It was not a princess's body, she was sure. It wasn't growing in the right places. She envied her younger sister's breasts, her straight auburn hair. She attacked hers with a brush and did not begin to count until she had done at least two hundred strokes. She was appalled when one of her sister's boy-friends tried to kiss her.

"Why?" she demanded.

The boy didn't know why. He had expected to be accepted or refused, not examined.

"Because you're pretty. . . ."

He said it like a question. Shell turned and ran. The grass seemed suddenly white, the trees white. She dropped the flowers meant for the fountain because they were white and dirty as bones. She was a spider on a field of ash.

"Primavera," said Breavman when he heard the story. "Not Botticelli – Giacometti."

"You won't let me keep anything ugly, will you?"

"No."

Besides, Breavman could not resist adding to his memory

the picture of a delicate American girl running through the woods, scattering wild flowers.

Shell loved the early morning. She asked for the room with the big east window which had been the nursery. She was allowed to choose her own wallpaper. The sun crept over the calico bedspread. It was her miracle.

Apparently life was not all Robert Frost and *Little Women*.

One Sunday morning she was in her mother's bed. They were listening to a children's programme. Gobs of snow, the size of seeded dandelions, were drifting diagonally across the many-paned windows. Shell's hair, gathered by a black ribbon, lay tame and smooth over her chest. Her mother was fingering it.

On the air a child was singing a simplified aria.

"Daddy's so silly. He says you're all growing up so fast that the house will be too big."

"He'll never leave his fish and chickens."

Her mother's fingers had been leisurely twining and intertwining but now only the thumb and forefinger were at work, a few strands of hair between them. The movement was that with which the bargain hunter tests the fabric of a lapel, but more rhythmical and prolonged.

She was smiling faintly and looking straight into Shell's face but Shell could not make contact with her eyes. The movement made the hair impersonal. It didn't belong to Shell. The blanket was moving. With the other hand her mother was doing something beneath it. The same rhythm.

There is a kind of silence with which we respond to the vices, addictions, self-indulgence of people close to us. It has nothing to do with disapproval. Shell lay very still, watched the snow. She was between the snow and her mother, unconnected to either.

The announcer invited all the boys and girls out there to join the Caravan next week, when they would take a trip to the far-off land of Greece.

"Well, aren't we the lazy things? Up you get, Miss Dainty. . . ."

Shell took a long time getting dressed. The house felt very ancient, haunted by the ghosts of old sanitary napkins, exhausted garters, used razor blades. She had encountered adult weakness with none of the ruthlessness of a child.

When her father, coming in red and jolly from walking in the woods, kissed her mother, Shell watched very closely. She was sorry for her father's failure, which she understood was as much a part of him as his passion for miniature houses, his gentle interest in animals.

It was not too many years before her mother began to exercise the inalienable rights of menopause. She took to wearing a fur coat and sun-glasses in the house at all times. She hinted, then claimed that she had sacrificed a career as a concert pianist. When asked on whose behalf, she refused to reply and turned the thermostat lower.

Her husband kept her eccentricities on the level of a joke, even though her attacks on her young daughters were occasionally vicious. He allowed her to become the baby of the house, kissing her as usual before and after every meal.

Shell loved him for the way he treated her mother, believed herself lucky to grow up in this atmosphere of married affection. His patience, his kisses were tiny instalments on a debt she knew he could never cover.

A damaging consequence of this neurotic interlude was a rivalry between Shell and her sister. Their mother developed and encouraged it with that faultless instinct which people who live under one roof have for one another's pain.

"I can't remember which of you hurt most," she reflected. "Good thing you weren't twins."

Shell's father drove her to school every morning. It was his idea that the girls go to different schools. This was a wonderful part of the day for both of them.

She watched the forest go by. She knew how happy he was

that she had inherited his love of trees. This was more important than her own delight, and it ushered her into a woman's life.

He drove very carefully. He must have been unwilling to turn his head to look at her, he had such a precious cargo. He mustn't have quite believed he had anything to do with her, she was so lovely, and he must have wondered why she believed the things he told her. When she was sixteen he gave her a car of her own, a second-hand Austin.

The school was a continuation of the house. There were many trees and trimmed bushes, many weathered buildings or buildings constructed to appear weathered. The enrolment represented an impressive concentration of old money, so no one could accuse the authorities of pretensions when they disguised the new junior residence with an Early American façade.

Its curriculum was not designed to produce artists, revolutionaries, or ceramicists. A Wall Street version of the little red schoolhouse, it trained girls to ornament society rather than question or subvert it.

Shell was formal. She sat on the grass with a book in front of the library and arranged her dress over her knees.

Let us say the dress was white and the book one of the interminable dialogues of Ivy Compton-Burnett, and let us say that this time her hair was bound in braids

If she wished to think about something she laid the book down carefully and leaned on one arm; perhaps with one finger she absently turned a page.

She knew she represented something immortal, she was sure. She was the girl in front of the building. Her age in the foreground, her fifteen-year-old body, her hair in the intermittent wind, were instruments to praise the weather and the old stones. She knew this, so she composed her face.

She must be still so that the unknown elderly man crossing the other side of the quadrangle, if he happened to glance

towards where she was sitting, would see the perfect thing, th
quiet thing, the girl before the preserved doorway, the scen
the heart demanded. It was her responsibility. Therefore sh
was serious, and the world was crumbling into plastic.

She loved the horizontal afternoon light. It seemed to com
right out of the shrubbery, and, for precious minutes, righ
out of the ground itself.

She must find a way to sit in that light.

2

Breavman was furious. He didn't want to move the bed. H
wanted to climb into it, hold her, and go to sleep.

They had driven all day. He didn't know where they were
probably Virginia, and he didn't know the name of the touris
house.

The woodwork was brown and perhaps the loose circu
wallpaper hid sinister bugs. He was too tired to care. The las
hundred miles her head had slept on his shoulder and h
vaguely resented her defection from the ordeal of the road

"What does it matter where the damn bed is? We'll be ou
of here by eight in the morning."

"I'll move it myself."

"Don't be silly, Shell."

"We'll be able to see the trees when we wake up."

"I don't want to see the trees when we wake up. I want t
look at the dirty ceiling and get pieces of dirty plaster grape
vine in my eye."

The ugly brass bed resisted her. For generations of sleeper
it had not changed its position. He imagined a grey froth o
dust on the underside. With a sigh he presented himself at th
other end.

"I offered to drive," she said to excuse her energy.

But he couldn't bear to be conducted through the night

helpless by the side of the speeding driver. If he had to find himself hurtling down a highway, neon motels and hamburgers arresting him absurdly like those uncertain images that were always flashing in his mind, he himself wanted to be in charge of the chaos.

"Besides, there's something irreverent about moving this stuff around."

She pushed hard, knuckles white on the brass bars.

It struck Breavman that they were the hands of a nun, bleached, reddened by convent chores; he had always thought them so delicate. Her body was like that. At first she might be mistaken for a *Vogue* mannequin, tall, small-breasted, angular, and fragile. But then her full thighs and broad shoulders modified the impression and in love he learned that he rode on a great softness. The nostrils of her face over-widened just far enough to destroy the first impression of exquisite harmony and allow for lust.

Her remarkable grace was composed of something very durable, disciplined and athletic, which is often the case with women who do not believe they are beautiful.

Yes, Breavman thought, she would have moved it with or without me. She is the Carry Nation of Evil Chintzy Rooms and I am the greasy drunkard smirking over my stack of Niagara Falls souvenirs. She learned to wield her axe three hundred years ago, clearing a New England field for planting.

Now the bed was beneath the window. He sat down and called for her with two open hands. They held each other softly and with a kind of patience as if they were both waiting for the demons developed in the silence of the long trip to evaporate.

At last she stood up, a little too soon, he thought.

"I've got to make the bed."

"Make the bed? The bed is perfectly well made."

"I mean at the other end. We won't be able to see anything."

"Are you doing this deliberately?"

He was surprised at the hatred in his voice. Nothing had evaporated.

She turned her eyes to him, trying to get through. I must read what she wants to say to me, I love them so much, he thought in a flash, but his anger overwhelmed him. He looked at the baggage to threaten her.

"Lawrence, this is where we are. This is our room for tonight. Just give me five minutes."

She worked quickly, a kind of side-to-side harvest dance, and the sheets flew as if they were part of her own dress. He knew that only she could change the chore into a ritual.

She puffed the pillows where their heads would lie. She removed one of the blankets and draped it over a hideous armchair, reshaping it with a few tucks and folds. Into the closet she lifted a small drum table complete with doilies, vase, and a broken trick box from which a scissor-beaked bird was meant to dispense cigarettes. She opened the wicker basket he had bought her and withdrew their books, which she placed carelessly on the large table beside the door.

"What are you going to do about the sink? There are cracks in the porcelain. Why don't you pry up a couple of floorboards and hide it under the carpet?"

"If you'll help me."

He would have liked to rip it from the wall and cause it to disappear with a magician's flourish, a white cigarette gone, a gift for Shell. And he would have liked to wrench it from its grimy roots and swing it like a jawbone, completely demolish the room which she had begun to ruin.

Shell put out his shaving kit and her own secret case of cosmetics which smelled of lemon. She opened the window with a little touch of triumph, and Breavman could hear leaves moving in the spring night.

She had changed the room. They could lay their bodies in it. It was theirs, good enough for love and talk. It was not that she had arranged a stage on which they might sleep hand in hand, but she had made the room answer to what she believed their love asked. Breavman knew it was not his answer. He wished he could honour her home-making and hated his will to hurt her for it.

But didn't she understand that he didn't want to disturb an ashtray, move a curtain?

One small light was burning. She stood in the shadows and undressed and then slipped quickly under the covers, pulling them up to her chin.

It's a better room for her, Breavman thought. Anyone else would have thanked her. She deserved a goose-feather bed with the sheets turned down so bravely-O. Which I cannot give her because I do not want the castle to cover it, with my crest carved above the hearth.

"Come."

"Should I close the light?"

"Yes."

"Now it's the same room for the both of us."

He got into the bed, careful not to avoid touching her. He knew his mood had to be attacked. Like the chronic migraine sufferer who doubtfully submits himself to the masseur who always cures him, he lay stiffly beside her.

She had known his body like this before. Sometimes he would disappear for two or three days and when he came back his body would be like that, armoured, distant.

Sometimes a poem would catapult him away from her, but she learned how to approach him, equipped with what he had taught her about her body and her beauty.

It was a refusal to be where he was, to accept the walls, the clock, the number on the door which he knew, the familiar limited human being in the familiar limited chair.

"You would have preferred it even dirtier," she said softly. "Maybe even roaches in the sink."

"You never see them if you keep the light on."

"And when the light is off you can't see them anyway."

"But it's the time between," Breavman said with developing interest. "You come home at night and you switch on the kitchen light and the sink is swarming black. They disappear in seconds, you do not follow too closely exactly where they go, and they leave the porcelain brighter than you ever imagined white could be."

"Like that haiku about strawberries on the white plate."

"Whiter. And without music."

"The way you talk you'd think we had fought our way out of the deepest slum."

"We have, but don't ask me to explain or it will sound like the cheapest nonsense from an over-privileged bourgeois."

"I know what you mean and I know that you're thinking I can't possibly know."

She would reach him, he was certain. She would uncover him so he could begin to love her.

"The mansion is as much a part of the slum as your horrible sink. You want to live in a world where the light has just been switched on and everything has just jumped out of the black. That's all right, Lawrence, and it may even be courageous, but you can't live there all the time. I want to make the place you come back to and rest in."

"You do a wonderful job of dignifying a spoiled child."

It was not that things decay, that the works of men are ephemeral, he believed he saw deeper than that. The things themselves were decay, the works themselves were corruption, the monuments were *made* of worms. Perhaps she was his comrade in the vision, in the knowledge of strangerhood.

"You didn't want to touch a thing when we came in here. You just wanted to clear a small corner to sleep in."

"Love in," Breavman corrected.

"And you hated me for remaking the bed and putting us where we could see the trees and hiding the ugly old table because all of that meant that we couldn't simply endure the filth, we had to come to terms with it."

"Yes."

He found her hand.

"And you really hated me because I was dragging you into it and you would have been free if you'd been alone, with morning a few hours away and the car parked outside. . . ."

God, he thought as he turned to her and closed her eyes over all he remembered of her, she knows everything.

3

Miss McTavish was a tall, mannish Bryn Mawr graduate, '21, who secretly believed that she was the only one in America who really understood the poetry of Gerard Manley Hopkins.

She also believed that the academic world was not worthy of the true Hopkins and was therefore reluctant to discuss her theories. The same superiority kept her out of the universities. She did not wish to participate in the donnish conspiracy against Life and Art.

The same superiority plus a grotesque nose kept her out of marriage. She knew that the man sufficiently intense, wild, and joyous for communion with her would be unavailable for domestic life, having in all probability already consecrated himself to the monastery or mountain climbing.

She saved her passion for the poems she read in class. Even the most cynical students knew that something very important was happening in those moments when she seemed to forget them most. Shell listened like a disciple, knowing that the poems were all the more beautiful because Miss McTavish had such a funny nose.

Miss McTavish liked to think of the Neo-Gothic library as her private home. On the way to the card index she floated over the bent heads, like a hostess presiding at a feast.

One evening, standing underneath the tall stained-glass windows, she said something very strange to Shell. The glass images could not be seen, only the bumpy lead separators. If mahogany wood could be made translucent and used as a filter, that was the colour of the light in the large quiet room. It was winter and Shell had the impression that snow was falling, she wasn't sure, not having stepped out since late afternoon.

"I've been watching you, Shell. You're the only aristocrat I have ever met." Then her voice choked. "I love you because I wanted to be like you, that's all I ever wanted."

Shell reached out her hand as if she had just seen someone wounded in front of her. Miss McTavish recovered instantly from her state of exposure and seized Shell's extended hand and shook it formally, as though they had just been introduced. Both of them bowed slightly several times, and it appeared to an observer that they might be just about to begin a minuet. The image they made occurred to both of them and they laughed in relief.

It was snowing. Without speaking they agreed on a walk. The pine trees beyond the Quadrangle were dark, lofty, and narrow as the windows in the library, shelves of snow on the limbs separating them from the night into rows of upright fish skeletons.

Shell felt that she was in a museum of bones. She had no sense of the outdoors at all, but imagined herself in a sinister extension of the library. And she was already summoning the resources of pity on which she knew she would have to draw.

Miss McTavish whistled a part from a quartet.

The quartet ended in a gasp.

"I've never done this before."

Shell stood still as she was kissed on the mouth, and caught the man's smell of alcohol on her teacher's breath. She tried to think through the present, reach the real forest she drove through with her father, but she couldn't.

"Ha ha," cried Miss McTavish, flinging herself backwards in the snow. "I'm brave. I'm very brave."

Shell believed her. She was a human tossed in the snow,

humiliating herself. She must be brave, as nuns with whips are brave, and drunk sailors in a storm. People who walk into desolation, beggars, saints, call to those they leave behind, and these cries are nobler than the victory shouts of generals. She knew this from books and her house.

Not too far away there was a second-class road. The headlights of a single car sawed through the woods, disappeared, and left the woman and the girl with a renewed sense of the outside, regulating world, which Shell already knew was engineered against the remarkable.

Miss McTavish had succeeded in immersing herself almost entirely in a drift of snow. Shell helped her out of it. They faced each other as they had in the library. Shell knew that her teacher would have preferred to be standing back there now, the declaration and kiss undone.

"You're old enough for me to say nothing."

Breavman was surprised to learn that Shell still corresponded with her.

"Once or twice a year," said Shell.

"Why?"

"I spent the rest of my time at school trying to convince her that she hadn't destroyed herself in my eyes and was still my ordinary and well-beloved English teacher."

"I know that kind of tyranny."

"Will you let me send your book to her?"

"If your idea of charity is to bore a Hopkins expert."

"This isn't for her."

"You'll wind up your debt –"

"Yes."

"– by becoming what she wanted you to be."

"In a way. I have a king."

"Ummm."

He was not convinced.

4

When Shell was nineteen she married Gordon Ritchie Sims. As the announcement in *The New York Times* specified, he was in the graduating class at Amherst and she was in her freshman year at Smith.

The best man was Gordon's room-mate, a devout Episcopalian whose banking family was of Jewish origin. He was half in love with Shell himself and dreamed of just such a wife to guarantee and cement his assimilation.

Gordon wanted to be a writer and most of his courting was literary. He enjoyed the fat letters he sent her from Amherst. Every night, after he had done a respectable amount of work on his thesis, he filled his personalized writing sheets with promises, love, and expectation, the passion tempered by an imitation of the style of Henry James.

Mail became a part of Shell's heart. She carefully chose the places to read these lengthy communications, which were far more exciting than the chapters of a novel because she was the major character in them.

Gordon summoned a world of honour and order and cultivation, and the return to a simpler, more exalting way of life which Americans had once experienced, and which he, by virtue of his name and love, intended to resurrect with her.

Shell loved his seriousness.

At the football weekends she practised being quiet beside him, indulging herself in the pleasures of responsible devotion.

He was tall and white-skinned. Horn-rimmed spectacles turned to pensive a face which without them would have been merely dreamy.

At dances their quiet behaviour and head-bending interest

in just about everything gave the impression that they were chaperons rather than participants in the celebration. One almost expected them to say, "We like to spend some time with young people, it's so easy to lose contact."

With him Shell passed from the startling colt-like beauty of her adolescence directly into that kind of gracious senility typified by Queen Mothers and the widows of American presidents.

They announced their betrothal in the summer, after a session of mutual masturbation on the screened porch of the Sims house at Lake George.

They married and after his graduation he immediately began his military service. It occurred to her as she drove him to the railway station that he had never really seen her completely naked, there were places he hadn't touched her. She attempted to conceive of this as a compliment.

She did not see very much of him in the next two years, weekends here and there, and generally he was exhausted. But his letters were regular and tireless, not to say disturbing. They seemed to threaten the serenity of a temporary widowhood she had been quite willing to assume.

She loved her clothes, which were dark and simple. She enjoyed the frequent extended visits at the houses of his family and hers. And she felt her place in the world: her lover was a soldier.

She would almost have preferred not to cut the envelopes. Intact, thick, lying on her dresser, they were part of the mirror in which she was brushing her long hair, part of the austere battered colonial furniture they had begun to collect.

Opened, they were not what he promised. They had become intricate invitations to physical love, filled with props, cold cream, lipstick, mirrors, feathers, games where the button is found in private places.

But on those weekends when he managed to get back to

their small apartment, he was too tired to do anything but sleep and talk and go to small restaurants.

The letters were not mentioned.

5

Shell believed her breasts were stuffed with cancer.

The doctor told her to put her blouse back on.

"You're a healthy woman. And lovely." He allowed that he was old enough to say that.

"I feel so foolish. I don't know where the bumps have gone."

Meanwhile, back at the Montreal poem factory, Breavman is interning, training to become her Compleat Physician.

6

After Gordon got out of the service they decided to move to New York and took a fairly expensive apartment on Perry Street in the Village. He had a job with *Newsweek,* in the books section, and he also sold some pieces to the *Saturday Review.* Shell was Girl Friday to one of the editors of *Harper's Bazaar.* She took some pleasure in refusing the many invitations to model.

According to their friends they had a cunning apartment. There was a tall handless clock with wooden works and roses painted on the face. There was a massive corner cabinet with many square glass windows in which they kept liqueurs and long-stemmed glasses. They had worked hard to remove the paint and stain it.

A child in severe clothes on a black background, painted by a journeyman portraitist, hung over a refectory table and insured the dignity of their frequent small dinner parties.

They were all good children eating up their frozen cream of shrimp soup, and they were about to assume control of the banks, the periodicals, the State Department, the Free World.

At one of these occasions, Roger, Gordon's old room-mate, managed to have a few private words with Shell. He had been liberated by six cognacs.

"If this ever stops working," – the gesture of his hand took in the accumulated triumph of antique shops – "come to me, Shell."

"Why?"

"I love you."

"I know you love me, Roger." She smiled. "And Gordon and I love you. I mean why should it ever stop working?"

Shell was holding an empty silver tray and he could see her face in it through the crumbs.

"I don't love you gently, friendly, I don't love you auld lang syne, I don't love you sweetheart of Sigma Chi." He had made it humorous enough; now he said seriously, "I want you."

"I know."

"Of course you do."

"No," she said, grateful for the tray she was holding. "Not the best friend."

"You can't be happy."

"Oh?"

There was something wrong with his suit, the pants hung badly, he would kill his tailor, the kitchen was too small, he wasn't elegant.

"He never touches you."

"How can you say this to me?"

"He told me."

"What?"

"It was the same all through school. He can't."

"Why? Tell me why!"

Now information was the most important thing. Apparently Roger thought she would kiss him for it, having been trained in trade. He found himself with his nose against the bottom of the silver platter.

"He can't, that's all. He can't. He never could. All you people are a laugh," he added, speaking from his authentic background.

7

How can anybody take the skyscrapers seriously? Breavman wonders. And what if they lasted ten thousand years, and what if the world spoke American? Where was the comfort for today? And each day the father's gift grows heavier – history, bricks, monuments, the names of streets – tomorrow was already crushed!

Where was the comfort? Where was the war to make him here and hero? Where was his legion? He had met people with numbers branded on their wrists, some of them wrecked, some shrewd and very quiet. Where was his ordeal?

Eat junk, join the enemies of the police, volunteer for crime? Correct America with violence? Suffer in the Village? But the concentration camps were vast, unthinkable. They seemed to descend on man from a great height. And America was so small, man-made.

In his room in the World Student House, Breavman leans elbows on the window-sill and watches the sun ignite the Hudson. It is no longer the garbage river, catch-all for safes, excrement, industrial poison, the route of strings of ponderous barges.

Can something do that to his body?

There must be something written on the fiery water. An affidavit from God. A detailed destiny chart. The address of his perfect wife. A message choosing him for glory or martyrdom.

His room is in the tower, beside the elevator shaft, and

he listens to the heavy mechanism of cables and weights. The mechanism of his pumping hand is just as ponderous. The glare off the Hudson is monotonous. There is a pigeon on Grant's Tomb. It's cold with the window open.

8

Gordon and Shell talked. Gordon welcomed the talk because again it was a literary treatment of the problem. And because they had labelled their absent bodies a problem, defined the boundaries of their trouble, they were able to bandage their union for a little longer.

As Gordon put it, they had a good solid house, why demolish it because one of the rooms could not be entered? They were intelligent people who loved each other; certainly a key could be found. And while they worked sanely for a solution they must not neglect the appointments of the other rooms.

So the well-ordered existence continued, really it flourished. Shell changed her dressmaker, Gordon moved his politics farther to the right. They bought a piece of land in Connecticut which had on it a sheep fold which they intended to preserve. Architects were consulted.

Shell was genuinely fond of him. She had to resort to that expression when she examined her feelings. That sickened her because she did not wish to dedicate her life to a fondness. This was not the kind of quiet she wanted. The elegance of a dancing couple was remarkable only because the grace evolved from a sweet struggle of flesh. Otherwise it was puppetry, hideous. She began to understand peace as an aftermath.

Now it seemed she was as tired as he was. The dinner parties were ordeals to be faced. The house was a huge project. They had to be in the country every other weekend and the traffic out of the city was impossible. And it was better to buy now because next year the prices would be even higher. The big things they stored but the apartment was crammed with cookie moulds, candle moulds, shoemaker benches, wooden buckets, and a spinning wheel which was too fragile for them to let out of their sight.

Shell grew to believe, in the terms of Gordon's metaphor, that they were living in a ruin already and that the locked door was the sole entrance to sanity and rest. But Gordon had taken pains to package the problem neatly not so much in order to examine it as to drop it into the sea. He was not one of those hairy passion chaps, it was not his nature, he almost believed, except, like all of us, he dreamed. In dreams the truth is learned that all good works are done in the absence of a caress.

A woman watches her body uneasily, as though it were an unreliable ally in the battle for love. Shell studied herself in the mirror, which had an eighteenth-century frame.

She was ugly. Her body had betrayed her. Her breasts were fried eggs. It didn't matter what she knew about Gordon, the extent of his responsibility in the failure. It was the burden of flesh and bone and hair which she could not command perfectly. She was the woman, the bad flower, how could he be blamed?

Look at the size of her thighs, they spread frighteningly when she sat. Gordon was tall, thin, white, her legs must weigh more than his legs. The appendix scar was an appalling gash ruining her belly. Damn the butcher doctor. And Gordon must be forgiven for not coming close to a dried wound.

Desire made her close her eyes, not for Gordon, not for a prince, but for the human man who would return her to her envelope of skin and sit beside her in the afternoon light.

Her friends had their problems too. Someone dedicated her seventh martini to the extinct American male. Shell did not raise her glass; besides, she didn't like hen parties. The toast-mistress regretted the death of American peasants, gamekeepers, and mourned the dependable cab-drivers, stable-boys, milkmen lost to analysts and psychological Westerns. Shell was not heartened by the general masculine failure.

What were the dressmakers doing? Why were all these massaged limbs bound in expensive cloth? A massage is not a caress. The intricate styles of hair, sleeves slit to show the arm, the children's eyes redeemed in pencil, what for? Whom to delight? Dead under the velvet. The rooms cleverly appointed, the ancient designs on the wallpaper, furniture of taste, rescued Victorian opulence, what was it meant to enclose? The beginning was wrong. The coupling did not occur. It should grow from entwined bodies.

The bath filled up. She nursed her body in, squatting on her knees, then, spreading her hands over the surface of the water as one does over a heater in a cold room, she slid back, even wetting her hair, wholly given over to the warmth and the dainty clean smell of lemon soap.

9

The crowd mounted the stone steps quickly. Perhaps when they reached street level their lives would have changed, roads gold, different homes and families waiting.

Two men moved faster than the crowd and the crowd let them through. Their lives were not outside the tunnel.

Breavman climbed at another speed, studying graffiti, wondering what secretary he could separate for the afternoon from her office routine. He had nowhere to go. He had abandoned the lectures he usually attended at that hour ever since the famous professor had agreed to let him do the term thesis on Breavman's own book.

"Stop!"

At least it sounded like stop. Breavman stopped but the command was not for him.

"Brother!"

He wished he understood their language. Why did he think he knew what the words were? The two men were fighting on the steps, wedging Breavman against the wall. He extracted his feet with difficulty, like someone stepping out of quicksand.

It took two seconds. They hugged each other tightly. There was a hollow grunt, Breavman could not be sure from which man. Then one stood up and ran. The other's head hung over the edge of the step less muscularly than a head should. The throat was widely and deeply cut.

Several voices shrieked for the police. A man who had the air of a doctor kneeled beside the body, which was already soaked in blood, shook his head philosophically to indicate that he was used to this sort of thing, then got up and went away. His attention had quieted the crowd, which was now beginning to bottleneck the passage, but after he had disappeared for some moments the cries for the police were renewed.

Breavman thought he should do something. He took off his jacket, intending to cover the victim, not the face, perhaps the shoulders. But what for? You did this for shock. The slit throat was past shock. It was softly bleeding over the IRT steps at the corner of Fourteenth Street and Seventh Avenue. At exactly one o'clock in the afternoon. Poor lousy urban matador. The white-on-white tie nattily knotted. The brown and white shoes very pointed and recently polished.

Breavman folded the jacket over his arm. It would implicate him. The police would want to know why he draped his jacket over a corpse. A bloody jacket was not a good idea for a souvenir. Sirens from the street. The crowd began to break up and Breavman went with it.

A few blocks away Breavman reflected that two years before he would have done it. A small death, like discovering that you can no longer slip into old underwear or ting the bell with the wooden mallet.

Why wasn't he thinking about the man?

Two years ago he would have dipped the jacket, made the gesture, connected himself with the accident. Was the ritual dissolving? Was this an advance from morbidity?

A vision of Nazi youth presented itself. Rows and rows of the gold heads filing past the assassinated soldier. They lowered their company flags into the wound and promised. Breavman swallowed bile.

A steady underground question persisted. Who was the man? Sometimes the question was obscured into Where did he buy the shoes? and From what corner did he flash them? Who was the man? Was he the man asleep in the subway at three in the morning dressed in a brand-new suit with scuff marks over the white part of his shoes? Did girls like his blue hair tonic? What shabby room did he step out of, glittering like the plastic madonna on the dresser? Who was the man? Where was he climbing? What was the quarrel, where was the girl, how much was the money? The knife into what water from what foggy bridge? Barry Fitzgerald and the rookie cop want to know everything.

Why wasn't he thinking about the man?

Breavman supported himself against a trash basket and vomited. A Chinese waiter ran out of the restaurant.

"Do it up the street. People eat here."

Puking clears the soul, he thought as he walked away. He was walking with all his body, which was newly light, easy with athletic promise. You're filled with poison, it's brewing in every pouch and hole and pocket of your insides, you're a swamp, then the sickening miracle, sloof! And you're empty, free, begin again your second cold clear chance, thank you, thank you.

The buildings, doorways, sidewalk cracks, city trees shone bright and precise. He was where he was, all of him, beside a dry-cleaning store, high on the smell of clean brown-wrapped clothes. He was nowhere else. In the window was a secular bust of a man with a chipped plaster shirt and a painted tie. It didn't remind him of anything when he stared at it. He was wildly happy to be where he was. Clean and empty, he had a place to begin from, this particular place. He could choose to go anywhere but he didn't have to think about that because here he was and every free deep breath was a beginning. For a second he lived in a real city, one that had a mayor and garbage men and statistical records. For one second.

Puking clears the soul. Breavman remembered what he felt like. Fry's Stationery, buying school supplies. Ten years old. The whole new school year coiled like a dragon to be conquered by sharp yellow Eagle pencils. Fresh erasers, rows of them, crying to be sacrificed for purity and stars for Neatness. The stacks of exercise books dazzlingly empty of mistakes, more perfect than Perfect. Unblunted compasses, lethal, containing millions of circles, too sharp and substantial for the cardboard box that contained them. Grown-up ink, black triumphs, eradicable mistakes. Leather bags for the dedicated trek from home to class, arms free for snowball or chestnut attacks. Paper clips surprisingly heavy in their small box, rulers with markings as complicated and important as a Spitfire's dashboard, sticky red-bordered labels to fasten your name to anything. All tools benign, unused. Nothing yet an accomplice to failure. Fry's smelled newer than even a winter newspaper brought in after the thump on the porch. And he commanded all these sparkling lieutenants.

Puking clears the soul but the bad juices come back quick. New York got lost in Breavman's private city. Gauze grew on everything and as usual he had to imagine the real shape of things. He no longer felt the light Olympic candidate. The painted plaster bust reminded him of some religious statues in a window a few blocks back. They were gaudy, plastic, luminous, sort of jolly. The bust was old, unclean, the white the colour of soiled therapeutic stockings. He tried to spit out the taste in his mouth. The plaster shirt, the sky, the sidewalk, verything was the colour of mucus. Who was the man? Why didn't he know the folklore of New York? Why didn't he remember that article about the particular trees which they planted in cities, hardy ones that withstood the polluted air?

He took the wrong Seventh Avenue subway. When he climbed to the street he noticed everyone was black. It was too complicated to get out of Harlem. He hailed a taxi to get him back across town. At World Student House the Puerto Rican elevator man conducted the creaky machine to the eleventh floor. Breavman wished he could understand the words to the song he was singing. He decided he would say *gracias* when he left the elevator.

"Watch your step."

"Thanks," said Breavman in perfect English.

He knew he'd hate his room before he unlocked the door. It was exactly the same as he'd left it. Who was the man? He didn't want to look out the window where General and Mrs. Grant were, or Gabriel on the roof of Riverside Church, or the shining Hudson, alien and boring.

He sat down on the bed, holding the key tightly in his right hand in exactly the position it had been when he twisted it in the keyhole, biting the inside of his cheek with molars. He was not really staring at the chair but the chair was the only image in his mind. He didn't move a muscle for forty-five minutes. At that point it occurred to him in a wave of terror that if he didn't make a great effort to rouse himself he would sit there forever. The maid would find him frozen.

Down at the cafeteria the fast-moving short-order man called him back for change.

"Giving it away, Professor?"

"No, I need it, Sam."

"Name is Eddy, Professor."

"Eddy? Glad to meet you, Sam."

I'm cracking up, thought Breavman. He was wet-eyed happy because of the trivial exchange. He sat at a small table, his hands clasped over the cup of tea, enjoying the warmth. Then he saw Shell for the first time.

Fantastic luck, she was sitting alone, but no, here was a man coming to her table, balancing a cup in each of his hands. Shell stood up to take one from him. She has small breasts, I love her clothes, I hope she has nowhere to go, prayed Breavman. I hope she sits there all night. He looked around the cafeteria. Everyone was staring at her.

He pressed his thumb and forefinger in the corners of his eyes, his elbow on the table – a gesture he always regarded a phony. The war-lined desk colonel signing the order that sends the boys, his boys, on the suicide mission, and then we see him steeled for the casualty lists, and all the secretaries have gone home, he is alone with his pin-studded maps, and maybe a montage of the young men in training, close-up of young faces.

Now he was sure. It was the first thing in a long time he had learned about himself. He wanted no legions to command. He didn't want to stand on any marble balcony. He didn't want to ride with Alexander, be a boy-king. He didn't want to smash his fist across the city, lead the Jews, have visions, love multitudes, bear a mark on his forehead, look in every mirror, lake, hub-cap, for reflection of the mark. Please no. He wanted comfort. He wanted to be comforted.

He grabbed the bunch of napkins out of the tumbler, wiped the excess ink from his ballpen on a corner of one of them, and scribbled nine poems, certain that she would stay as long as he wrote. He shredded the napkins as he dug the pen in, and he couldn't read three-quarters of what he'd done; not that it was any good, but that had nothing to do with it. He stuffed the debris into his jacket and stood up. He was armed with amulets.

"Excuse me," he said to the man with her, not looking at her at all.

"Yes?"

"Excuse me."

"Yes?"

Maybe I'll say it ten more times.

"Excuse me."

"Can I help you?" A little anger showing. The accent was not American.

"May I – I would like to talk to the person you are with." His heart was driving so hard he could believe he was transmitting the beats like a time signal before the news.

The man granted permission by turning up the palm of his open hand.

"You're beautiful, I think."

"Thank you."

She didn't speak it, her mouth formed the words as she looked at her loosely clasped hands composed at the edge of the table like a schoolgirl's.

Then he walked out of the room, grateful it was a cafeteria and he had already paid his bill. He didn't know who she was or what she did but he had no doubt whatever that he would see her again and know her.

10

Shell took a lover at the end of her fifth year of marriage. It was shortly after she started her new job. She knew what she was doing.

Talking with Gordon had failed. He was only too eager to talk. She wanted them both to go to psychiatrists.

"Really, Shell." He smiled at her paternally, as if she were an adolescent reciting the *Rubaiyat* with too much belief.

"I mean it. The insurance covers it."

"I don't think it's necessary," he understated, meaning that it was the most outrageous thing he had ever heard of.

"I do."

"I've read Simone de Beauvoir," he said with gentle humour. "I know this world is not kind to women."

"I'm talking about us. Please talk with me. Don't let this night go by."

"Just a second, darling." He knew that at this precise moment she was challenging him to a solemn meeting. He suspected that it was the last time she would ever confront him like this. He also knew that there was nothing within himself that he could summon to meet her. "I really don't think you can characterize our lives together as a catastrophe."

"I don't want to characterize anything, I want –"

"We've been pretty lucky." His brand of humility took in the apartment, Shell's closet of dresses, the plans for the second floor of the house, which were laid out on the desk and to which he was anxious to return.

"Do you want me to thank you?"

"That wasn't becoming." He allowed her to know he was angry by speaking with a slight British intonation. "Let's try to understand the process of marriage."

"Please!"

"Don't get hysterical on me. Oh, come on, Shell, let's grow up. A marriage changes. It can't always be passion and promises. . . ."

It never was. But what was the use of shouting that? He fictionalized an early storm of flesh and wildness from which they had matured. He believed it or he wanted her to believe it. She would never forgive him for that dishonesty.

". . . thing we have now is extremely valuable . . ."

Suddenly she didn't want the doctors, didn't want to save anything. She watched him speak with that terrible scrutinizing attention that can make a stranger of a bed-mate. She felt that he spoke to her from a far distance. She was a cub reporter in the audience. It was too late for easy married mumbling or intimate silence. He knew she was pretending to be convinced, was grateful to her for the pretence. What else could she do – weep, burn down the walls? She was in a room with him.

Later she said, "Well, where should we put the partition?" and they leaned over the house plans, playing house.

Breavman often reviews this scene. Shell told it to him a year later. He sees the two of them bending over the oiled desk, backs towards him, and he sees himself in the corner of the antique room, staring at the incredible hair, waiting for her to feel his gaze, turn, rise, come to him, while Gordon works with his sharp pencil, sketching in the bathroom, the insult of a nursery. She comes to him, they whisper, she looks back, they leave. And in some of the versions he says, "Shell, sit still, build the house, be ugly." But her beauty makes him selfish. She has to come.

When she decided to change her job Gordon thought it was a good idea. She was glad to get back into the academic atmosphere. It was a tracking-back, Gordon said. She could re-establish her bearings. Shell simply couldn't stand another day at *Harper's Bazaar*. Watching the cold bodies, clothes.

A friend of hers was doing a couple of afternoons a week of voluntary work at World Student House, hostessing at teas for foreign students, hanging decorations, showing America at its smiling prettiest to the future ministers of black republics. She informed Shell that there was a job open in the Recreation Department. Since a friend of the family was a director and benefactor of the organization her application and interview were formalities. She moved into a pleasant green office decorated with UNESCO reproductions, which looked over Riverside Park, much the same view as Breavman's, though less elevated.

She did her work well. The Guest Speakers Programme, the Sunday Dinner Programme, the Tours Programme were better run than they had ever been. She emerged as an expert organizer. People listened to her. Perhaps a creature that lovely wasn't supposed to speak such sense. Nobody wanted to disappoint her. Success terrified her. Perhaps this was what she was meant to do, not love, not live close. Nevertheless, she liked working with students, meeting people her own age who were planning and beginning their careers. She walked into the spring atmosphere, she found herself making plans.

It was strange how friendly she felt to Gordon. The construction of the house was fascinating. Every detail interested her. They rented a truck to pick up panelling from an old country hotel which was being demolished. Gordon saw his study in oak. Shell suggested one full wall for the living-room, the other three left in brick. She was puzzled by her own concern.

Then it occurred to her that she was leaving him. Her interest was exactly the kind displayed to a cousin with whom one has grown up and whom one does not expect to see again for a long time. One clamours to hear everything about the family – for a little while.

When she slept with Med it was merely the signature to a note of absence she had been writing for almost a year.

He was a visiting professor from Lebanon, a remarkably handsome young man who was an expert in these matters, who, in intimate circumstances, would admit to his companion that the constant proximity of "desirable little things" was what most attracted him to the academic life. He was over six feet, thin, hair black and carefully wild and swept back, eyes black and always slightly squinted as if he were looking over stretches of sand for high deeds to perform. He was a T. E. Lawrence Bedouin with an Oxford accent and theatrically exquisite manners. He was always so obviously on the make, so captivated by his charm and indisputable good looks, so dedicated to his vocation, so phony that he was altogether delightful.

Shell allowed him to court her extravagantly for three

weeks. He was not in his best form because he really believed her beautiful and this intruded on the perfection of his technique.

He gave her a filigree brooch shaped like a scimitar which he claimed belonged to his mother but which she wouldn't have accepted if she hadn't been sure he travelled with a bag of them. She accepted a transparent black nightgown like the ones advertised in the back of *Playboy*, the kind he seriously believed every American girl coveted – she was delighted with his naïveté.

Deprived of sweet sexual fiat for so long, indeed never having known it, she righteously defended the privilege to make herself sick. And because he was so pretty, so absurd, nothing she did with him could be serious or important. What she knew was going to happen would not really have happened. Except that she needed the dynamite of adultery to blast her life, destroy the rising house.

Over whose hips was she pulling the flimsy black costume? She could see her hair through the material.

In the mirror of a bathroom in the hotel on upper Broadway. Steel-rimmed, round-cornered mirror. Whose body?

Med had reserved the room for a week. The critical week. He had never spent so much money on an adventure.

The bathroom was brilliantly clean. She had been frightened that it would have a naked bulb on a cord, cracked porcelain, hair on old soap. *Is this Shell?* she inquired blankly of her image, not because she wanted to know, or even open the subject, but because that question was the only form her modesty could assume.

At first Med couldn't speak. He had made a mistake, for men of his character the most painful mistake, occurring once or twice in a lifetime and crushing the heart: he might have loved her. The room was dim. He had arranged the lighting, tuned his transistor radio to the classical-music station. She seemed to create her own silence, her own shadow to stand in. She was not part of his setting.

"Isn't that the Fifth?" he said finally.

"I don't know."

She knew which symphony it was. The answer she spoke was in response to the question before the mirror.

"I believe it is. Da, da da da da. Of course it is."

She wished he would begin.

She felt no desire. This both pleased and pained her. Desire she would hoard for a lover. Med was not her lover. Desire would have made what she was doing important, and it was not important, it must not be important. A weapon, yes, but not a special night in her heart. Not with this clown. Yet, and this was the pain, he was a man and surely she should long for only someone to hold her after all this time. She had dreamed love, bites, surrender, but all she felt now was interest. Interest! Perhaps Gordon was her true mate after all.

Med relied on a Peeping Tom survey of her body to inflame him.

It fascinated her to see a man overwhelmed with desire.

Oh Shell, cries Breavman as he learns of the hotel, as she tells him in the voice she uses when she must tell him everything. Shell, fly away. Heap flowers in the stone fountain. Fight with your sister. Not you with the Expert Fool, in a room like the ones Breavman built. Not you who wore white dresses.

As Med lay beside her, silently cataloguing what he had gathered, Shell succumbed to a wave of hatred which made her grit her teeth. She did not know where to attach it. First she tried Med. He was too simple. Besides for the first time since she had known him he seemed genuinely sad, not theatrically melancholy. She guessed he was walking through a museum of dead female forms. She absently massaged the nape of his neck. She tried to hate herself but all she could hate was her silly body. She hated Gordon! She was here because of him.

No, that was not true. But still she hated him and the truth of this threw open her eyes, wide in the dark.

She inspected herself as she dressed. Her body seemed an interesting alien twin, a growth which she didn't own, like a wart on one's finger.

Breavman bites his lip as he listens.

"I shouldn't tell you this," Shell says.

"Yes."

"It wasn't me. It wasn't the me you're holding now."

"Yes it was. It is."

"Does that hurt you?"

"Yes," he says, kissing her eyes. "We have to bring everything to each other. Even the times we are corpses."

"I know what you mean."

"I know you do."

If I can always decipher that, Breavman believes, then nothing can happen to us.

Armed with the betrayal, Shell approached her husband.

One needs weapons to hunt those close. Foreign steel must be introduced. The world in the married house is too spongy, familiar. The pain, present in plenty, is absorbed. Other worlds must be ushered in to cut the numb.

Gordon was running hot water over a box of strawberries. He knew it would happen like this. Auden had said so. After her first few words he seemed not to hear what she said. He had always known that this was the way it would come.

He answered, "I see" and "Of course I understand" and "I see" several more times. He kept his hand between the hot and the cold. Preserving the colourful wrapper intact assumed great importance.

Then suddenly she was leaving him. His life was changing right now.

"I want to live by myself for a little while."

"A little while?"

"I don't know how long."

"In other words it could be a very long time."

"Perhaps."

"In other words you have no intention of returning."

"I don't know, Gordon. Can't you see I don't know?"

"You don't know but you have a pretty good idea."

"Gordon, stop. You won't get anything out of me like that. You never have."

At this point it occurred to Shell that when she had begun to speak to him she had not intended to leave but to give him a last chance.

"Stay here."

He turned off the tap, pushed the box with deliberation into a corner of the sink as though it were a chessman, and wiped his hands. It was an ugly voice he used. The words were less than a plea and more than a proposition.

"Stay. Don't break up our marriage over this."

"Is it so little?"

"Women have affairs," he said without philosophy.

"I was with a man," she said incredulously.

"I know." And the softer: "It's not the end of the world."

But she wanted it to be the end of the world. She wanted a mark on the forehead to prove the union was rotten. That he was fighting for his life was difficult for her to perceive. She interpreted his speech as part of his daily affront. Now he wanted to formalize the disaster.

"I won't interfere. I won't ask you questions."

"No."

He thought she was bargaining.

"You'll get it out of your system. You'll see, we'll weather this."

"No!"

He never understood to what she was shouting "No."

Even men of limited imagination can sometimes imagine the worst. So he could not have been really surprised to see her packing one day, or to hear themselves discussing who would

take what bureau, what candle-mould, or to find himself on
the telephone making arrangements with movers to save Shell
the trouble. For years now he had known he didn't deserve
her; it was a matter of time. Now it was happening and he had
already imagined his gentlemanly role.

Shell visited her parents in Hartford. They still lived in the
big white house, just the two of them. Officially they regretted
the separation and hoped she'd soon return to her husband
and her senses. But she had a long talk with her father as they
walked over the property. The leaves were drained of green
but they had not yet turned bright. She was surprised how easily she was able to talk to him.

"He had no right," was all he said about Gordon, but it was
a handsome old man speaking, who had lived out some kind
of man's life, and it fortified her.

He let her talk, inviting it with his silence and the paths he
chose. When she was through he spoke about the first growth
of some trees he had planted.

She could not help feeling that her mother regarded the
break-up as a sinister triumph of heredity, like haemophilia in
a royal child that had seemed too healthy.

Shell was lucky to be able to rent a small apartment on 23rd
Street. She didn't want to get too far from the Village. Except
for a tiny kitchen, bathroom, and vestibule, she lived in one
room. She stood the tall clock beside the entrance to the main
room. She painted the walls lavender and threw lavender
translucent draperies over the windows, which seemed to eth-
erize the light, make it thin, and perfume the air with cool
colour.

It was not her home in the same way her body was not her
own. She merely lived in them. She watched herself move
among the pretty things. She didn't believe that she was the
proper woman to have such a good career job, or to leave a
husband or to entertain a lover. It horrified her.

She would not see Med again, of course, and one afternoon

in the cafeteria she told him why. She was not created for a minor adventure. Their interview was interrupted by a young man whose curious declaration moved her unreasonably.

Breavman thought about her all the time but he experienced no lust for her. This was new. He thought about her presence with no longing. She was alive, her beauty existed, she was pulling on her gloves or pushing back her hair or staring at a movie with her huge eyes. He did not want to tear down the theatre in his fantasy and rescue her from the dark fiction. She was there. She was in the city, or some city, some train, some castle or office. He knew their bodies would move together. That was the least of it.

He didn't think of himself as a lover. He knew they would lie mouth to mouth, happier, safer, wilder than ever before. One of the comforts of her merely being was that he need make no plans.

Once or twice he told himself that he ought to find her, ask people. It wasn't necessary. He was willing to enter into homage whether he saw her again or not. Like a Wordsworthian hero, he did not wish her his.

He didn't even remember her face too perfectly. He hadn't studied it closely. He had lowered his head and dug his pen into napkin poems. She was what he expected, was always expecting. It was like coming home at night after a tedious extended journey. You stand a minute in the vestibule. No light is switched on. He didn't have to explore her features. He could walk blindfolded into praise of her, once the first open armourless glance guaranteed her beauty.

It was the very last time Breavman let go the past and hard promises which he could barely articulate. He did no writing. He suspended himself in the present. He read an architectural survey of New York City and was surprised at his capacity for concentration and interest. He listened to lectures without thinking about the professor's ambition. He built a kite. He strolled through Riverside Park without coveting the solitary nurses or growing the destinies of children in toy racers. The trees were fine as they were, losing their leaves, both Latin and common names unknown. There wasn't much terror in the old women in black coats and lisle stockings sitting on the benches of upper Broadway, or the mutilated vendors of pencils and plastic cups. He had never been so calm.

He spent many evenings in the Music Room of World Student House. Thick blue carpet, wood panelling, dark heavy furniture, and a sign commanding quiet. The record collection was only adequate but it was all discovery for him. He had never really listened to music before. It had been a backdrop for poems and talk.

Now he listened to other men. How they spoke! It made his own voice small and put his body back into the multitudes of the world. No images formed while he listened, nothing he could steal for his page. It was their landscape where he sat guest.

He was following the flute in a Schubert quartet. It climbed and returned and ascended again, launched and received by low powerful strings. Shell opened the door, stepped into the room, turned to the door to give her attention to closing it softly. She quickly crossed the silent carpet and sat in a chair beside the french windows, through which she could see the darkening park, walls, and street.

He noticed the way she tried to relax her body, to make herself like a child hearing a favourite story. But her hands tightened on the carved wooden arms and for a hundredth of a second she was suffering in an electric chair. Then she sank back again and tried to annihilate herself in the melody.

Some women possess their beauty as they do a custom sportscar or a thoroughbred horse. They drive it hard to every appointment and grant interviews from the saddle. The lucky ones have small accidents and learn to walk in the street, because nobody wants to listen to an arrogant old lady. Some women wear moss over their beauty and occasionally something rips it away – a lover, a pregnancy, maybe a death – and an incredible smile shows through, deep happy eyes, perfect skin, but this is temporary and soon the moss re-forms. Some women study and counterfeit beauty. Industries have been established to serve these women, and men are conditioned to favour them. Some women inherit beauty as a family feature, and learn to value it slowly, as the scion of a great family becomes proud of an unusual chin because so many distinguished men bore it. And some women, Breavman thought, women like Shell, create it as they go along, changing not so much their faces as the air around them. They break down old rules of light and cannot be interpreted or compared. They make every room original.

He believed she was in some kind of pain, or rather, defeat. The loveliness she composed seemed to rebel and escape her, as sometimes a poem under the pen becomes wild and uncontrollable. This did not modify his wonder at her. What she created was still remarkable. Into that he wouldn't dare intrude. But perhaps he could have some part in comforting her.

She recognized him and met his stare, having learned that this was the best method to greet the public seducer, and immediately perceived that there was in his eyes nothing that tried to make her an indifferent means, an object. She was simply being adored. For some curious reason she remembered a certain dress she had worn when she was at school and wished vaguely to be wearing it or know where it was. His head was inclined, he was smiling. He's ready to watch me all night, she thought. Not speak, not ask anything. She wondered who he was. His face was young but there were unusually deep lines from his nostrils to the corners of his mouth. It was as if all his experience were recorded there. The mouth would have been too full and sensual without the chastening lines, like those idiotic fat kissing lips of Hindu gods.

Well, what was she doing thinking about his lips? And what

was she doing in this chair sitting so stilly for him? She should be back at her apartment, thinking, considering her future, learning a language, sorting things out, or whatever people who live alone are supposed to do when they come back at night.

She realized that years ago this was exactly how she would have liked to be observed, with music, before a window, with light made soft by old wood.

Soon she wouldn't be able to see the separate stones in the wall, or the iron fence against the bushes. The sidewalks were mother-of-pearl, and although she could not see it, she knew the sun was dragging darkness as it cut behind the rose-edged New Jersey hills. Would he never turn away?

She closed her eyes and could still feel his stare. It had the power of defenceless praise. It did not call her beautiful, but called her to delight in her beauty, which is more understandable and human, and it pleased her to contemplate the pleasure she created. Who was the man who did this to her? She opened her eyes and smiled her curiosity at him. He stood up and walked to her.

"Will you come with me?"

"All right."

"It's almost dark."

They left the room softly. Breavman closed the door carefully. They exchanged their names in whispers and laughed when they remembered that they could talk out loud.

They walked back and forth on the cement expanse that stretches in front of Grant's Tomb. There is a certain formality about that area; at night it could be the private garden of an illustrious friend. They went in step over the large squares.

"The Grants are excellent hosts," said Shell.

"They retire very early of an evening," said Breavman.

"Wouldn't you say their house is a wee bit pretentious?" said Shell.

"That's generous. The entrance hall looks like a bloody mausoleum!" said Breavman. "And I hear he drinks."

"So does she."

They joined hands and ran down the hill. Crisp leaves splintered under their feet and they looked for drifts of them to trample down. Then they watched the traffic speed on the driveway below, the lights of countless cars. On the Hudson there were other lights, the necklace of the George Washington bridge, the slow-moving barges and the Alcoa sign across the water. The air was clear, the stars big. They stood close and inherited everything.

"I must go now."

"Stay up the night with me! We'll go to the fish market. There are great noble monsters packed in ice. There are turtles, live ones, for famous restaurants. We'll rescue one and write messages on his shell and put him in the sea, Shell, seashell. Or we'll go to the vegetable market. They've got red-net bags full of onions that look like huge pearls. Or we'll go down to Forty-second Street and see ten movies and buy a mimeographed bulletin of jobs we can get in Pakistan –"

"I work tomorrow."

"Which has nothing to do with it."

"But I'd better go now."

"I know this is unheard of in America, but I'll walk you home."

"I live on Twenty-third Street."

"Exactly what I'd hoped. It's over a hundred blocks."

Shell took his arm, he brought his elbow close against her hand, and they were both part of a single motion, a sort of gentle Siamese beast that could cover ten thousand blocks. She took her arm away after a little while and he felt empty.

"Is there something wrong?"

"I'm tired, I guess. There's a cab."

"Talk to me a second before we get into a car."

She thought it was too difficult to explain. He would

onsider her a perfect fool of a possessive female if she told im. She didn't want to walk that close to anyone casually. nd was the man supposed to declare himself after knowing er for half an evening? And she didn't even know her own esires; he was a stranger. Of one thing only she was certain. he could not expend herself in the casual.

"I'm married," was all she said.

He studied her face. It was a temptation not to connect her oveliness with prosaic human problems. All her expressions ere so beautiful, what did it matter what provoked them? Weren't her lips perfect when they trembled? Then he remem- ered the pain he had sensed in her when she was sitting efore the window. He shook his head and answered her.

"No, no, I don't think you are."

He hailed a taxi and before he could touch the handle of the loor the cabbie leaned over and pushed it open. Times Square vas a sudden invasion of light. Blue veins showed through the kin of their faces and hands and the bald head of the driver. hey welcomed the comparative darkness of Seventh Avenue. hey weren't close enough yet to enjoy ugliness.

He told the cab to wait and took her to the elevator.

"I won't ask you up," Shell said without coyness.

"I know. We have time."

"Thank you for saying that. I loved our walk."

He dismissed the taxi and walked the hundred blocks him- elf. Trying not to step on cracks was the extent of any ordeal e entertained. He had retired into comfort, which is doing vhat you know you can do.

Shell got ready for bed quickly. When she was lying in the lark she suddenly realized that she hadn't brushed her hair.

11

Breavman always envied the old artists who had great and ccepted ideas to serve. Then the colour of gold could be laid

on and glory written down. The death of a god in scarlet an
glowing leaf is very different from the collapse of a drunkar
in a blue café, no matter what underground literature migh
profess.

He never described himself as a poet or his work as poetr
The fact that the lines do not come to the edge of the page is n
guarantee. Poetry is a verdict, not an occupation. He hated t
argue about the techniques of verse. The poem is a dirt
bloody, burning thing that has to be grabbed first with bar
hands. Once the fire celebrated Light, the dirt Humility, th
blood Sacrifice. Now the poets are professional fire-eater
freelancing at any carnival. The fire goes down easily an
honours no one in particular.

Once, for a while, he seemed to serve something other tha
himself. Those were the only poems he ever wrote. They wer
for Shell. He wanted to give her back her body.

> Beneath my hands
> your small breasts
> are the upturned bellies
> of breathing fallen sparrows.

Or was it really for her that he worked? It made it easier fc
him if she liked her body. The bed was more peaceful. The
didn't begin as poems at all, but propaganda. The verdict wa
poetry. If she continued to believe her flesh an indifferer
enemy then she would not let him look at her as he wante

He would fold the sheet away from her to watch her whil
she slept. There was nothing in the room but her uncovere
flesh. He didn't have to compare it with anything. To kne
beside her and run his fingers on her lips, follow every shap
was to annihilate sunsets he couldn't touch. Ambitio
demands of excellence were happily lost as he rested in he
This was most excellent. But she had to feel herself whole.
goddess mustn't fidget. So he must work to make her joyou

and still. She learned the conventional instrument of climax, which for a woman is the beginning of pride and stillness.

When she finally shyly traded her body with his she wasn't altogether certain that she wouldn't disgust him. Gordon had said he loved her but he had refrained from touching her. Five years. He had allowed limited contact. Not her body but the fingers of one hand might trace his furtive dash to pleasure. Her flesh died from that. Every night it went greyer.

Breavman brushed aside the silk like a cobweb fallen across her shoulders. She made a little noise of pleasure and resignation, as if now he knew the worst. He rested his head on her breast, this old attitude speaking best for him.

She learned quickly, but no woman is so beautiful she will not want her beauty told again in rhyme. He was a professional, he knew how to build a lover to court her.

He thought poems made things happen. He had no contempt for the robot lover who made every night a celebration and any meal they took a feast. He was a skilful product, riveted with care, whom Breavman wouldn't have minded being himself. He approved of the lover's tenderness, was even envious of some of the things the lover said, as though he were a wit Breavman had invited for dinner.

The lover, being planned so well, had a life of his own and often left Breavman behind. He came to Shell with his gift, let us say, of an ostrich feather bought at a Second Avenue store or tea roses from the shops at the corner of Eighth Street. He sat at Shell's table and they exchanged gossip and plans.

> Wherever you move
> I hear the sounds of closing wings
> of falling wings
>
> I am speechless
> because you have fallen beside me
> because your eyelashes
> are the spines of tiny fragile animals.

"They cashed a cheque for me at the supermarket."

"The privileges of beauty. The last high caste left in classless America."

"No, they did the same for a little brown old lady."

"So the neighbourhood virtues persist."

"How did your work go?"

"I blackened my page."

> I dread the time
> when your mouth
> begins to call me hunter.

The chatter went on and on. Stories of Hartford, the stone fountain, the summers at Lake George, huge houses remembered. Stories of Montreal, night drives with Krantz, death of a father. And as they lived together their own stories grew, myths of first meeting, first loving, quiet of coming trips.

"Can I read you something?"

"Yours?"

"You know I can't stand anybody else's work."

She wanted him to sit beside her in a special favourite way.

"Is it about me?"

"Well, wait till I read the damn thing."

She listened seriously. She asked him to read it again. She had never been so happy. He began in his low voice which always abdicated before the meaning of the words, never forced an effect. She loved this honesty in him, this intensity that made everything important.

"Oh it's fine, Lawrence, it's really fine."

"Good. That's what I wanted."

"But it's not for me – it's not for anyone."

"No, Shell, it's for you."

She had a treat for him, frozen strawberries.

> When you call me close
> to tell me
> your body is not beautiful

> I want to summon
> the eyes and hidden mouths
> of stone of light of water
> to testify against you.

Breavman watched his deputy make her happy while he stared and stared. One night he watched her while she slept. He wanted to know what happened to her. Some faces die of sleep. Mouths go limp. Gone eyes leave a corpse behind. But she was whole and lovely, her hand close to her mouth and clutching a corner of sheet. He heard a cry in the street. He crept to the window but he could see nothing. The cry sounded like the death of something.

> I want them
> to surrender before you
> the trembling rhyme of your face
> from their deep caskets.

I don't care who's being killed, he thought. I don't care what crusades are being planned in historical cafés. I don't care about lives massacred in slums. He searched the extent of his human concern beyond the room. It was this: cool condolence for the women less beautiful than she, for the men less lucky than he.

Because he was attached to magic the poems continued. He didn't realize that Shell was won not by the text but by the totality of his attention.

"Can I come in?"

"No."

"Why?"

"I'm getting dressed."

"Precisely."

"Don't come in, please. You're going to get horribly tired of me. All the books say I'm supposed to guard my mystery."

"I want to watch you get mysteriously dressed."

It was not strange that she interpreted this devotion to her presence as love.

> When you call me close
> to tell me
> your body is not beautiful
> I want my body and my hands
> to be pools
> for your looking and laughing.

12

Shell decided to go through with the divorce. Gordon acquiesced. He had intended to put up a battle but when she visited him at his office he was intimidated by her. She was so quiet and friendly, inquiring about his work, happy for his success. She referred to the marriage tenderly, but was firm about its ending, as though it were an after-supper game in the twilight but now the children had to come home to bed. He did not have to guess at the source of her strength. Except for one afternoon when they were filling out some final papers and he made a last-ditch effort to keep her, he was happy he'd had the luck to spend five years with her. And in a few years his literary disposition, unrequited by *Newsweek*, would allow him to dramatize himself to younger women with this little tragedy.

"This is between me and Gordon," she said to Breavman. Like general lovers, they could only speak in each other's arms. "So don't go getting your hat."

They had lived together for almost a year. She didn't want him to regard the divorce as a signal to propose. Of course she wanted to marry him. She was not equipped for lovers, for her idea of love was essentially one of loyalty, a loyalty grounded in passion.

Sometimes she believed that no one could give so much tenderness, attention, except as an investment in the future.

Sometimes she knew, she could locate the pain in her heart, that he could give so much only if he was going away.

She had already given everything to him, a bestowal we make only once in our lives. She wanted him to love her freely. That is most of the total gift. She had also been bred in the school of hero-martyrs, and saw herself, perhaps, as an Héloïse. Only the man of adventure could love – that was his writing – and only the lady who had abandoned her house and name – that was conventional society. Adventurers leave the couch, ladies return to their name; this knowledge is the ordeal which keeps the clasp tight.

It isn't often we meet someone who has the same vision of what we might be as we have for ourselves. Shell and Breavman, or rather his deputy, saw each other with this remarkable generosity.

She came in crying one afternoon. He took her gloves and purse, put them on the oiled-wood commode, led her to the green sofa.

"Because of what I told Gordon."

"You had to tell him."

"Not everything I did. I'm terrible."

"You're a terrible vicious witch."

"I told him how good it is with you; I didn't have to do that. I just wanted to hurt him."

They talked all night until Shell could declare, "I hate him."

Breavman observed to himself that she was further from divorce than she thought. Women take very seriously an attempt to mutilate their bodies. Breavman did not understand that as soon as she uttered the words in his arms she was free from hatred.

He was bothered by the knowledge that Shell was making real decisions, acting, changing her life. He wanted to watch her at rest. It involved him in the world of houses and traffic lights. She was becoming an authentic citizen, using his love for strength.

Suppose he went along with her towards living intimacy, towards comforting incessant married talk. Wasn't he abandoning something more austere and ideal, even though he laughed at it, something which could apply her beauty to streets, traffic, mountains, ignite the landscape – which he could master if he were alone? Wasn't that why he stared at her, indulged himself in every motion, expression? Perhaps it was only the conviction that he wasn't created for comfort which disturbed him. Disturbed him because it was vanishing.

He was very comfortable. He had begun to accept his deputy's joy. This lover was the most successful thing he had ever made, and the temptation was to supply him with wallet and identification and drown the master Breavman in a particularly garbage-strewn stretch of the Hudson River.

The Breavman eye, trained for volcano-watching, heavenly hosts, ideal thighs and now perfectly at work on the landscape of Shell's body, was in danger of sleep. More and more the lover had Shell to himself. These are the times Breavman does not remember too well because he was so happy.

13

Summer was still very young.

Did you know forget-me-nots were that tiny?

They climbed the hill behind the cabin, listened to the birds, checked the guide to identify their calls.

He didn't want to give her the little flowers because they both listened to names so carefully.

They talked about the conduct of parting. This to lovers is as remote and interesting as a discussion of H-bomb defence at a convention of mayors.

"... and if it isn't working for one of us, we've got to tell the other."

"... and let's hope we have the courage to be surgical."

Shell was delighted by a certain cluster of birch.

"They look like *naked* trees! They make the woods look black."

At night they listened to the sound of the lake beating the sand and shore stones. A dark luminous sky made of burned silver foil. The cries of birds, wetter and more desperate now, as though food and lives were involved.

Shell said that every sound of the lake was different. Breavman preferred not to investigate; he enjoyed the blur of happiness. She could listen more carefully than he. Details made her richer, chained him.

"If you tape their whistles, Shell, and slow them down, you can hear the most extraordinary things. What the naked ear hears as one note is often in reality two or three notes sung simultaneously. A bird can sing three notes at the same time!"

"I wish I could speak that way. I wish I could say twelve things at once. I wish I could say all there was to say in one word. I hate all the things that can happen between the beginning of a sentence and the end."

He worked while she slept. When he heard her easy breathing he knew the day was sealed and he could begin to record it.

A queer distortion of honesty holds me back from you . . .

Shell made herself wake up in the middle of the night. Moths battered against the window beside which he worked. She crept behind him and kissed his neck.

He wheeled around in surprise, pencil in hand, and scraped skin from her cheek. He upset the chair as he stood.

They faced one another in the cold flat light of the Coleman lantern. The night was deafening. The whirring and thudding of the moths, the hiss of the lantern, the water working on boulders, small animals hunting, nothing was at rest.

"I thought I . . ." He stopped.

"You thought you were alone!" she cried in pain.

"*I thought I . . .*" "*You thought you were alone,*" he recorded when she was asleep again.

14

One night, watching her, he decided he would leave the ne
morning.

Otherwise he'd stay beside her always, staring at her.

It was the middle of June. He was running an elevator in
small office building, scab labour. He picked up extra mon
cleaning some of the offices on Friday evenings. It was a ricl
ety elevator, carried a maximum of five passengers, and we.
out of commission if brought too far below the basemei
floor level.

At night there was Shell, poems and the journal while sh
slept.

Most of the time he was happy. This surprised and di
turbed him, as generals get uneasy during a protracted peac
He enjoyed the elevator, which was sometimes a charic
sometimes a torture device of Kafka, sometimes a tin
machine, and, the worst times, an elevator. He told peop
who asked that his name was Charon and welcomed the»
aboard.

Then there were the evening meals with Shell. Straw ma
on an oiled-wood folding table. Candlelight and the smell
beeswax. The elaborate food lovers will prepare for or
another, cooked in wine, held together by toothpicks. C
hilarious gentle morning feasts out of cans and frozen boxe

There were weekend breakfasts of eggs and blueberry mu
fins when Shell was the genius of an ancient farmhous
kitchen histories away from New York – which they coul
abandon at any time for the green sofa, which was dateles
There were movie afternoons, mythological analyses of
Westerns, historic spaghetti dinners at Tony's at which th
phoniness of Bergman was discovered.

The poems continued, celebrating the two of them. Poem

f parting a man writing to a woman he will not let out of his
ght. He had enough for a fat book but he didn't need a book.
hat would come later when he needed to convince himself
hat he had lived such a life of work and love.

Breavman became his deputy. He returned to his watch-
ower an hour every few days to fill in his journal. He wrote
uickly and blindly, disbelieving what he was doing, like a
hrice-failed suicide looking for razor blades.

He exorcized the glory demons. The pages were jammed
nto an antique drawer that Shell respected. It was a Pandora's
ox of visas and airline-ticket folders that would spirit him
way if she opened it. Then he would climb back into the
warm bed, their bodies sweetened by the threat.

God, she was beautiful. Why shouldn't he stay with her?
Why shouldn't he be a citizen with a woman and a job? Why
houldn't he join the world? The beauty he had planned as a
epose between solitudes now led him to demand old ques-
ions of loneliness.

What did he betray if he remained with her? He didn't dare
ecite the half-baked claims. And now he could taste the guilt
hat would nourish him if he left her. But he didn't want to
eave for good. He needed to be by himself, so he could miss
her, to get perspective.

He shoved an air-mail letter into the stuffed drawer.

He watched her sleeping, sheet clutched in her hand like an
amulet, hair sprung over the pillow in Hokusai waves. Cer-
ainly he would be willing to murder for that suspended body.
t was the only allegiance. Then why turn from it?

His mind leaped beyond parting to regret. He was writing
o her from a great distance, from some desperate flesh-
overed desk in the future.

My darling Shell, there is someone lost in me whom I
drowned stupidly in risky games a while ago – I would like to
bring him to you, he'd jump into your daydreams without
asking and take care of your flesh like a drunk scholar, with

laughing and precious secret footnotes. But as I say, he i
drowned, or crumpled in cowardly sleep, heavily medicated
dreamless, his ears jammed with seaweed or cotton – I don'
even know the location of the body, except that sometimes h
stirs like a starving foetus in my heart when I remember yo
dressing or at work in the kitchen. That's all I can write.
would have liked to bring him to you – not this page, not thi
regret.

He looked up from his lined book. He imagined Shell's sil
houette and his own. Valentine sweethearts of his parents
time. A card on his collector's shelf. Could he enbalm her fo
easy reference?

She changed her position, drawing the white sheet tigh
along the side of her body, so that her waist and thigh seemed
to emerge out of rough marble. He had no comparisons. I
wasn't just that the forms were perfect, or that he knew then
so well. It was not a sleeping beauty, everybody's princess. I
was Shell. It was a certain particular woman who had an
address and the features of her family. She was not a kaleido
scope to be adjusted for different visions. All her expression
represented feelings. When she laughed it was because. Wher
she took his hand in the middle of the night it was because
She was the reason. Shell, the Shell he knew, was the owner o
the body. It answered her, was her. It didn't serve him from a
pedestal. He had collided with a particular person. Beautifu
or not, or ruined with vitriol tomorrow, it didn't matter. Shel
was the one he loved.

When the room was half filled with sunlight Shell opened
her eyes.

"Hello," said Breavman.

"Hello. You haven't been to sleep at all?"

"No."

"Come now."

She sat up and straightened the bedclothes and pulled a

corner down to invite him in. He sat on the edge of the bed.
She wanted to know what was the matter.

"Shell, I think I should go to Montreal for a little. . . ."

"You're leaving?"

He felt her stiffen.

"I'll be back. Krantz is coming back – he wrote and offered
me this job at a camp. . . ."

"I knew you were leaving. For the past few weeks I could
just tell."

"This is just for the summer. . . ."

"How long?"

"The summer."

"How many months?"

Before he could answer she brought her fingertips to her
mouth with a little hurt sound.

"What is it?" asked Breavman.

"I sound like Gordon did."

He took her in his arms to tell her this wasn't the same thing
at all. She recalled him to their promise to be surgical.

"That's nonsense, you know it is. C'mon, let's create a great
breakfast."

He stayed that day and the next, but the third day he left.

"Really, Shell, it's just the summer."

"I haven't said anything."

"I wish you'd be more miserable."

She smiled.

Book IV

1

CONCERNING THE bodies Breavman lost. No detective will find them. He lost them in the condition of their highest beauty. They are:

a rat
a frog
a girl sleeping
a man on the mountain
the moon

You and I have our bodies, mutilated as they might be by time and memory. Breavman lost them in fire where they persist whole and perfect. This kind of permanence is no comfort to anyone. After many burnings they became faint constellations which controlled him as they turned in his own sky.

It might be said they were eaten by the Mosaic bush each of us grows in our heart but few of us cares to ignite.

2

He stood on the lawn of the Allan Memorial, looking down at Montreal.

Loonies have the best view in town.

Here and there were clusters of people gathered on the expensive grass around wood furniture. It could have been a country club. The nurses gave it away. White and perfect, there was one on the circumference of every group, not quite joining the conversation, but in quiet control, like a moon.

"Good evening, Mr. Breavman," said the floor nurse. "Your mother will be glad to see you."

Was that reproach in her smile?

He opened the door. The room was cool and dark. As soon as his mother saw him it began. He sat down. He didn't bother saying hello this time.

". . . I want you to have the house, Lawrence, it's for you so you'll have a place for your head, you've got to protect yourself, they'll take everything away, they have no heart, for me it's the end of the story, what I did for everyone, and now I have to be with the crazy people, lying like a dog, the whole world outside, the whole *world*, I wouldn't let a *dog* lie this way, I should be in a hospital, is this a *hospital*? do they know about my feet, that I can't walk? but my son is too busy, oh he's a great man, too busy for his mother, a poet for the world, for the world . . . !"

Here she began to shout. Nobody looked in.

". . . but for his mother he's too *busy*, for his shiksa he's got plenty of time, for her he doesn't count minutes, after what they did to our people, I had to hide in the cellar on Easter, they chased us, what I went through, and to see a son, to see my son, a traitor to his people, I have to forget about everything, I have no son. . . ."

She continued for an hour, staring at the ceiling as she ranted. When it was nine o'clock he said, "I'm not supposed to stay any longer, Mother."

She stopped suddenly and blinked.

"Lawrence?"

"Yes, Mother."

"Are you taking care of yourself?"

"Yes, Mother."

"Are you eating enough?"

"Yes, Mother."

"What did you eat today?"

He mumbled a few words. He tried to make up a menu she'd approve. He could hardly speak, not that she could hear.

". . . never took a cent, it was everything for my son, fifteen years with a sick man, did I ask for diamonds like other women. . . ."

He left her talking.

There was a therapeutic dance going on outside. Nurses held by frightened patients. Recorded pop music, romantic fantasies even more ludicrous in this setting.

When the swallows come back to Capistrano

Behind the circle of soft light in which they moved rose the dark slope of Mount Royal. Below them flashed the whole commercial city.

He watched the dancers and, as we do when confronted with the helpless, he heaped on them all the chaotic love he couldn't put anywhere else. They lived in terror.

He wished that one of the immaculate white women would walk him down the hill.

3

He saw Tamara almost every night of the two weeks he was in the city.

She had abandoned her psychiatrist and espoused Art, which was less demanding and cheaper.

"Let's not learn a single new thing about one another, Tamara."

"Is that laziness or friendship?"

"It's love!"

He staged a theatrical swoon.

She lived in a curious little room on Fort Street, a street of dolls' houses. There was a marble fireplace with carved torches and hearts, above it a narrow mirror surrounded by slender wood pillars and entablatures, a kind of brown Acropolis.

"That mirror's doing nobody any good up there."

They pried it out and arranged it beside the couch.

The room had been partitioned flimsily by an economical landlady. Tamara's third, because of the high ceiling, seemed to be standing on one end. She liked it because it felt so temporary.

Tamara was a painter now, who did only self-portraits. There were canvases everywhere. The sole background for all the portraits was this room she lived in. There was paint under her fingernails.

"Why do you only do yourself?"

"Can you think of anyone more beautiful, charming, intelligent, sensitive, et cetera?"

"You're getting fat, Tamara."

"So I can paint my childhood."

Her hair was the same black, and she hadn't cut it.

They founded the Compassionate Philistines one night and limited the membership to two. It was devoted to the adoration of the vulgar. They celebrated the fins of the new Cadillac, defended Hollywood and the Hit Parade, wall-to-wall carpets, Polynesian restaurants, affirmed their allegiance to the Affluent Society.

Wallpaper roses were peeling from the grapevine moulding. The single piece of furniture was a small Salvation Army couch, over-stuffed and severely wounded. She supported herself as an artist's model and ate only bananas, the theory of the week.

The night before he left she had a surprise for him and a loyal Compassionate Philistines. She removed her bandanna.

She had dyed her hair blonde in accordance with the aims of the organization.

Good-bye, old Tamara, Breavman recorded for his biographers, may you flourish, you have a three-hundred-thousand-dollar mouth.

4

When would the old dialogue with Krantz resume?

The lake was beautiful in the evening. Frogs went off like coiled springs.

When would they sit beside the water like small figures in a misty scroll painting, and talk about their long exile? He wanted to tell him everything.

Krantz lectured the counsellors on Indoor Games for Rainy Days. Krantz prepared a days-off schedule. Krantz set up a new buddy system for the waterfront and drilled the counsellors for two hours. Krantz carried a clip-board and a whistle around his neck.

No crude bugle wakened them in the morning, but a recording on the PA of the first few bars of Haydn's Trumpet Concerto. Krantz's idea. On the fifth morning of the pre-camp training programme which Krantz had instituted for the counsellors, Breavman knew that this particular piece of music had been ruined for him for life.

Well, Krantz was busy. And there was this girl, Anne, who had followed him from England. Thank God she wasn't beautiful. She was a modern dancer.

After the organization was completed and the kids arrived, things would run smoothly and they would repair their old commentary on the universe.

Krantz explained the American game of baseball.

"If a guy catches a ball after it's hit, the batter's out."

"That sounds rational," said Anne, and they hugged.

He hoped the dialogue would begin soon, because there was nothing he liked about camp. Obscene. He felt it the minute he arrived. There is something obscene about a rich kids camp. Something so obvious it disgusts. It's like an amusement park, like rows of elaborate pinball machines. He looked around at the playing fields, handball-courts, bunks, boats - receptacles to hold children for a summer, relieve parents Gangrene in the family. Living rooms back in Montreal were stinking with twisted intimacy.

He was glad that four hundred miles away Shell was waiting.

The counsellors were on the dock, lying in the sun. Breavman surveyed the flesh. Soon it would all be brown, bronze would grow around the bra straps. Now they were city-white How the pines must despise them!

Breavman looked at a tall girl named Wanda. She was sitting at the far end of the dock, dangling her toes in the water She had good legs and yellow hair but they didn't whip him She wasn't quite in the great golden tradition. Wanda, you're safe from Breavman.

All the girls were very plain. And this was the joke. He knew what two months in that community would do. He'd be writing sonnets to all of them. These poems-to-be made him tired

The Laurentian sky was jammed with stars. Breavman who didn't know the names of constellations, judged confusion to be an aspect of their beauty.

"Counsellors' meeting," Krantz called up to the balcony.

"Let's not go, Krantz."

"Brilliant idea, except that I'm chairman."

As they walked to the Counsellors' Lounge they were joined by Ed, a first-year law student at McGill.

"First guy to make it with Wanda gets it," Ed proposed. " mean, it's a matter of time. We're all going to make her before the summer's over, it happens every season, but this way one of us stands to collect."

Breavman hated that kind of young-buck talk. He wished he had the courage to smash his face. Maybe Krantz would do it. He was supposed to be a lover now.

"I suppose you're wondering how we can be certain when the first man claims the money." Ed, the legalist, explained the silence of the other two. Breavman searched the silence for their old unity.

"I think we can trust each other," said Krantz. "Breavman?"

Breavman called their attention to a falling star.

"A contract of cosmic significance."

They agreed that five dollars each would make the pool worthwhile.

What did you expect, Breavman, reunion on a windy hill, a knife ceremony and the exchange of blood?

5

The bus depot was a chaos of parents, children, fishing rods, tennis racquets, and bewildered dogs dragged to see their young masters away. Mothers who had been awaiting the great day for weeks were suddenly stricken with a certainty that their babies would starve without them. A special diet was pressed into Breavman's hand along with a five-dollar bill.

"I know you'll look after him," a woman shouted hurriedly, scanning the crowd meanwhile for someone else to bribe.

Fifteen minutes before the scheduled departure Breavman sneaked into one of the empty waiting buses. He closed his eyes and listened to the confusion beyond the window. What was he doing with these people?

"My name is Martin Stark. Capital *S*, small *t*, small *a*, small *r*, small *k*. No *e*."

Breavman wheeled around.

In the seat behind him, sitting very stiffly, was a boy of about twelve years. His eyes were incredibly white, not naturally, but as if he were straining to show as much white as possible. This gave him an expression of having just seen a catastrophe.

"Sometimes I spell it with an *e* and then I have to tear up the page and begin again."

He spoke in a monotone, but over-articulating each word as if it were an elocution lesson.

"My name is Breavman. Capital *B*, small *r*, small *e* . . ."

He had been warned about Martin, who was going to be one of his campers. According to Ed, Martin was half-nut, half-genius. His mother was supposed to be ashamed of him. At any rate she never came on Visiting Day. Today, Breavman learned from the boy, she had come an hour early and deposited him in the bus with the command not to stir. Thus she avoided meeting the other parents.

"I'm your counsellor this summer, Martin."

Martin registered no reaction to this information. He continued to stare beyond Breavman with a kind of vacant, unchanging terror. He had a bony face and a great Caesar nose. Because he generally clenched his teeth when he wasn't talking, the lines of his jaw were severely outlined.

"What's your favourite store?" asked Martin.

"What's yours?"

"Dionne's. What's your favourite parking lot?"

"I don't know. What's yours?"

"Dionne's Parking Lot."

The questions excited Martin because now he asked breathlessly, "How many windows are in the building Dionne's is in?"

"I don't know, Martin. How many?"

"In all the walls?"

"Of course all the walls. What good would it do to know the number of windows in only one wall or even three walls?"

Martin supplied a number triumphantly. Breavman

idiotically promised himself he would check next time he was in town.

"How many cars were in the Dionne's Parking Lot last Thursday?"

"Tell me."

Fifty campers invaded the bus. There was much scrambling and bargaining for seats and Breavman's rapport with the boy was lost. Martin sat calmly through the ride, mumbling to himself. Breavman learned later that he liked to give himself four-figure numbers to multiply together.

On the way north Breavman asked him, "Do you like the countryside?"

"After I investigate it."

6

Three hundred jaws make a lot of noise chewing together. The benches were always too far from or close to the table and needed complicated co-operative action to adjust. He almost slapped a camper for blowing bubbles in his glass of milk.

After the meal Breavman and Ed performed, Breavman pumping out intricate chords that he knew were lost and Ed ruining the high registers of his harmonica to rise above the general mess-hall din.

Breavman, who always wanted to hear Handel playing in his head, beat the wire strings of a borrowed guitar. He had no callouses to resist the bite of the strings on the fingers of his left hand.

His campers and Ed's shared a bunkhouse, and the counsellors had a partitioned area to themselves in the same wood building. They had between them decided on a policy of rigorous discipline for the first few days. Then they would ease off and be nice guys. After a stern talk the boys went to bed efficiently, except for Martin, who took half an hour to urinate. Ed told them to keep quiet in the morning no matter what time they got up.

The counsellors lay on their cots, the atmosphere of strict control hanging heavy. Martin's queer clipped voice rang out

"Can I make number two before line-up?"

"Yes, Martin."

"Can I clean my nose?"

"If it isn't a noisy operation."

"Can I write my brother?"

Ed leaned over and whispered to Breavman, "He has no brother."

When they were asleep he ran to the kitchen, where there was a telephone. He phoned Shell in New York. He wanted her voice to obliterate the day. He wanted to hear her say the word "darling". He had phoned her half a dozen times from the city and he owed a huge bill.

He gave nothing to her and waited, reading over and over the Telephone Company's printed instructions on how to dial a number. An interior voice was screaming: It doesn't work, it doesn't work.

Shell told him how much she loved Joseph Conrad.

They said good-bye softly, both of them knowing the three minutes had failed.

He wrote for two hours, describing the day in detail. The black-fly bites on his arm disturbed him and he put that down. His Indian jacket was too hot but he didn't feel like taking it off. He put that down.

7

Martin fascinated him. He reckoned that he had misinterpreted Martin's expression. It was not vacant terror but general wonder. He was that rarest creature, a blissful mad-child.

The other children understood his election and treated him with a kind of bemused awe.

One afternoon they entertained themselves by encircling Martin and firing large numbers at him to multiply.

He rocked back and forth, like a man at prayer, his eyes closed. He beat his thighs with open palms as he thought, like an awkward bird trying to leave the ground, and made a buzzing sound as though his mind were machinery.

"Em-m-m-m-m-m-m-m-m-m-m . . ."

"Look at him go!"

"Em-m-m-m-m-m-m-m-m-m-m . . ."

"C'mon, Martin boy!"

"Eighty-one thousand, nine hundred and eighteen," he announced, opening his eyes. The boys cheered and hugged him.

Then he caught sight of a small pine tree. He stopped dead, stared, and walked out of the circle. Breavman followed him.

"Are you okay?"

"Oh yes. I believe I'd better count these."

Until supper he amused himself by discovering how many needles there were on an average pine tree.

Krantz was annoyed when he discovered what Breavman's afternoon activity was.

"That isn't what Mrs. Stark pays her money for."

"No?"

It was incredible that they should have put themselves into a position where one could castigate the other.

"Not to have her son used as a side-show freak."

"What does she pay her money for?"

"Come off it, Breavman. You know it wasn't healthy. She wants the kid to be like everyone else – integrated, inconspicuous. It's hard enough on her as it is."

"Okay, we'll force him into baseball."

"Infractions of the regulations will be severely disciplined Herr Breavman."

8

A horse-shoe of hills rose behind the bunks. On one of the hills there was an amphitheatre with wooden benches and stage. It was used for plays, singsongs, and on Sabbath as a House of Prayer.

> How goodly are thy tents, O Jacob,
> and thy dwelling place, O Israel . . .

They sang in Hebrew, their voices mingling with the sunlight. It was fragrant there, the pines high, blasted, and black. The camp was assembled in white clothes.

That's how we are beautiful, he thought, that's the only time – when we sing. Storm troopers, band of crusaders, gang of stinking slaves, righteous citizens – only tolerable when their voices ring in unison. Any imperfect song hints at the ideal theme.

Ed told a wonderful Sholem Aleichem story about a young boy who wanted to play the fiddle but was forbidden to by his Orthodox parents. For a minute Breavman thought he would overdo it, but no, he swayed and danced under his imaginary fiddle and everyone believed him.

The same Ed who bet with a girl's body.

Breavman sat thinking that he could never do as well, never be so calm and magical. And that's what he wanted to be: the gentle hero the folk come to love, the man who talks to animals, the Baal Shem Tov who carried children piggyback.

He would never be able to pronounce a Jewish word with any confidence.

"Krantz," he whispered, "why weren't we allowed to cross the tracks?"

Twelve righteous faces told him to shh.

Still, and he knew it was arrogance, he often considered himself the Authentic Jew. His background had taught him the alien experience. He was grateful for that. Now he extended that experience to his own people.

What was it all about anyhow? A solitary man in a desert, begging for the inclination of a face.

Anne performed a Hasidic dance, annihilating anything womanly in her body with the crammed, ironic movements. But for a few moments they were lost in Europe, their skins untanned, waiting in narrow streets for miracles and the opportunity for revenge they would never take.

After the Sabbath services a butterfly seemed to follow him down the hill, disappearing as he left the wooded area for the hot campus. He felt the honour of it all through the day.

9

"It's so hard," said Shell's voice. "Everybody has a body."

"I know," Breavman said. "And there's one point in an evening when the thing most urgently needed is just an arm around the shoulder."

"I'm so glad we can still talk."

Her honesty obliged her to describe her temptations. She wanted to keep nothing from him. They both understood the danger of this technique: there are humans that desire me. Keep me or they will.

He leaned against the wall in the dark kitchen and listened. How curious that anyone should speak to him so softly! How had he managed to arrange the miracle in which someone spoke softly to him? It was a magic he was sure he never possessed, like reading one's first poems. But here was his own name whispered.

An ugly forecast developed in his heart that he would drive the whisperer to a hundred indifferent beds and silence her.

"Shell, I'm coming to New York tomorrow!"

"You're quitting camp?"

"There's nothing for me here."

"Oh, Lawrence."

It was raining when he went outside, her voice still with him. He began to circle one of the playing fields. The tall pines around the field and hills gave him the impression of a bowl which contained him. There was one black hill that seemed so connected with his father that he could hardly bear to look up at it as he came round and round, stumbling like a drunk.

The rain hazed the electric lights isolated here and there. An indescribable feeling of shame overwhelmed him. His father was involved in the hills, moving like a wind among the millions of wet leaves.

Then an idea crushed him – he had ancestors! His ancestors reached back and back, like daisies connected in a necklace. He completed circle after circle in the mud.

He stumbled and collapsed, tasting the ground. He lay very still while his clothes soaked. Something very important was going to happen in this arena. He was sure of that. Not in gold, not in light, but in this mud something necessary and inevitable would take place. He had to stay to watch it unfold. As soon as he wondered why he wasn't cold he began to shiver.

He sent Shell a funny telegram explaining why he couldn't come.

10

Breavman received a letter from Mrs. Stark, Martin's mother. It wasn't customary for parents to reply to the official reports the counsellors were obliged to send.

Dear Mr. Breavman,

I'm sure my son Martin is in excellent hands.

I'm not anxious and I don't expect any further detailed communications concerning his behaviour.

Very sincerely,

R. F. STARK

"What the hell did you write her?" demanded Krantz.

"Look, Krantz, I happen to like the kid. I took a lot of trouble over the letter. I tried to show that I thought he was a very valuable human being."

"Oh, you did?"

"What was I supposed to say?"

"Nothing. As little as possible. I told you what she's like. For two months of every year she doesn't have to look at him every day and can pretend that he's a normal boy doing normal things with other normal boys at a normal camp."

"Well, he isn't. He's much more important than that."

"Very good, Breavman, very compassionate. But keep it to yourself, will you? It was Breavman you were pleasing, not the boy's mother."

They were standing on the balcony of the Administration Building. Krantz was about to announce Evening Activity over the PA.

Didn't Krantz know what he knew about Martin? No, that wasn't true. He didn't know anything about the boy, but he loved him. Martin was a divine idiot. Surely the community should consider itself honoured to have him in their midst. He shouldn't be tolerated – the institutions should be constructed around him, the traditionally incoherent oracle.

Out in the open, tempered by the dialogue, it wouldn't sound so mad.

Krantz looked at his watch, which he wore on the inside of his wrist. As he turned to go in he caught sight of a figure lying face down in the darkness near a row of bushes at the bottom of the lawn.

"For God's sake, Breavman, that's the sort of thing I mean."

Breavman walked quickly across the lawn.

"What are you doing, Martin?"

"Twenty thousand and twenty-six."

Breavman returned to the balcony.

"He's counting grass."

Krantz shut his eyes and tapped the banister.

"What's your evening activity, Breavman?"

"Scavenger hunt."

"Well, get him over there with the rest of the group."

"He isn't interested in a scavenger hunt."

Krantz leaned forward and said with an exasperated smile, "Convince him. That's what you're supposed to be here for."

"What difference does it make whether he goes looking for yesterday's newspaper or counts grass?"

Krantz leaped down the stairs, helped Martin up, and offered him a piggy-back across the field, to where Breavman's group was assembled. Martin climbed on gleefully and as he rode stuck his index fingers in his ears for no apparent reason, squinting as if he were expecting some drum-splitting explosion.

Every night, just before he went to sleep, it was Martin's custom to declare how much fun he had had that day. He checked it against some mysterious ideal.

"Well, Martin, how did it go today?" asked Breavman, sitting on his bed.

The mechanical voice never hesitated.

"Seventy-four per cent."

"Is that good?"

"Permissible."

11

He marvelled at how still he could lie.

He was stiller than the water which took the green of the mountains.

Wanda was fidgeting, pretending to write a letter in what was left of the light of the day. So her long yellow hair wasn't quite in the great tradition. Her gold-haired limbs could be worshipped individually, but they did not amalgamate into beauty. Nevertheless, how many thighs could he kiss at the same time?

If I had a really immense mouth.

The flies were very bad. They put on Six-Twelve. Wanda extended her arm to him but instead of applying the lotion himself gave the bottle to her. His fantasy: applying the lotion with greater and greater frenzy all over her flesh.

A light rain swept across the face of the water, veiling it with a silver net. From time to time they heard the cheer of the camp, which had assembled in the mess hall for a Lassie movie.

The rain passed and the still surface recomposed itself.

"I've never really lived by a lake," said Wanda, who was given to walking barefoot.

"Now don't get into poetry, Wanda."

He absently caressed her face and hair, which was softer than he had imagined.

An inner eye flying away from the boathouse like a slow high star gave him the view of a tiny plywood box in which two minuscule figures (mating insects?) made inevitable ballet movements to each other.

Wanda was trying to get her head into a position in which she could kiss his caressing fingers.

Finally he kissed her lips, mouth, stomach, all the parts.

Then something very disturbing occurred.

Her face blurred into the face of little Lisa, it was dark in the boathouse, and that face blurred into one he didn't recognize, that one dissolved into the face of Bertha, maybe it was the blonde hair. He stared hard to make the changing stop, to return to the girl beside him.

He chased the different faces with his mouth, stopping no one. Wanda mistook his exercise for passion.

They walked back up the path. The sky was mauve. A moon emerged from a gentle accumulation of clouds. The path was softened by millions of pine needles. Martin would find out how many, perhaps.

Wanda sneezed. The damp wood planks.

"It was so peaceful down there, so peaceful."

Breavman was tempted to punish her for the trite rhythm of her sentence by telling her about the pool for her body.

"Do you know what the ambition of our generation is, Wanda? We all want to be Chinese mystics living in thatched huts, but getting laid frequently."

"Can't you say anything that isn't cruel?" she squeaked as she ran from him.

He sat up all night to punish himself for hurting her. The morning birds began. In the window grew a cool grey light, the trees beyond still black. There was a light mist on the mountain but he didn't feel like following it.

A few days later he discovered that he had caught Wanda's cold. And he couldn't understand the way his campers were shoving food down their faces. They bubbled in the milk, diluting it with spit, fought over extras, sculptured out of squeezed bread.

Breavman glanced at Martin. The boy hadn't eaten anything. Krantz had warned him that he must supervise the boy's diet closely. Sometimes he went on mysterious hunger strikes, the reasons for which could never be discovered. On this occasion Breavman could have hugged him.

His head was completely stuffed. The flies were vicious. He went to bed with the campers but couldn't sleep.

He lay there thinking stupidly of Krantz and Anne, lovingly of Shell.

The horizontal position was a trap. He would learn to sleep standing up, like horses.

Poor Krantz and Anne off in the woods. How long can they lie naked before the black flies get them? His hands will have to leave her flesh and hair to scratch his own.

"Can I come in?"

It was Wanda. Of course she could come in. He was fettered on the bed, wasn't he?

"I just want to tell you why I haven't let you see me."

She turned off the lights to give them an even chance against the flies. They mingled fingers as she talked. Just before he drew to himself and kissed her lightly, he noticed a firefly in the corner. It was flashing infrequently. Breavman was sure it was almost dead.

"Why are you kissing me?"

"I don't know. It's not what I came here for. Just the opposite."

He was taking a great interest in the firefly. It wasn't dead yet.

"Why the hell don't you know?"

She was fumbling with something under her blouse. "You've broken my bra strap."

"This is a great conversation."

"I'd better go."

"You'd better go. He'd better go. We'd better go. They'd better go."

"You can't seem to talk to anyone."

Was that supposed to make him miserable? It didn't. He had given himself to the firefly's crisis. The intervals became longer and longer between the small cold flashes. It was Tinker Bell. Everybody had to believe in magic. Nobody believed in magic. He didn't believe in magic. Magic didn't believe in magic. Please don't die.

It didn't. It flashed long after Wanda left. It flashed when Krantz came to borrow Ed's *Time* magazine. It flashed as he tried to sleep. It flashed as he scribbled his journal in the dark.

Boohoohoohoohoohoo say all the little children.

12

It was three in the morning and Breavman was glad they were all sleeping. It was tidier that way, the campers and counsellors arranged on their cots, row after row. When they were awake there were too many possibilities, egos to encounter, faces to interpret, worlds to enter. The variety was confusing. It was hard enough to meet one other person. A community is an alibi for the failure of individual love.

A clear night, cold enough to turn the breath to steam. The landscape seemed intimately connected to the sky, as if it were held in the grip of the high, icy stars. Trees, hills, wood buildings, even a low streak of mist, were riveted to the rock of the planet. It seemed that nothing would ever move, nothing could break the general sleep.

Breavman walked, almost marched, between the black-filled cabins. He was exhilarated to be the only free agent in this frozen world. Wanda was asleep, her hair colourless. Martin was asleep, his jaws relaxed, at home in his terror. Anne was asleep, a dancer out of training. Krantz was asleep. Certainly he knew how Krantz slept, how his lips budged forward each time he exhaled his jagged snore.

He dissolved the walls in his mind as he walked between them, and he took an inventory of each form's isolation. This night's sleep was strangely graceless. He noted the greedy expression a sleeper wears, that of a solitary eater at a banquet. In sleep every man is an only child. They turned, they shifted, drew up a limb, uncocked an elbow, turned again, shifted again, a series of prize crabs, each on his private white beach.

All their ambition, energy, speed, individuality was swaddled in excelsior, like rows of Christmas ornaments out of season. Each form, so intent on power, was locked in a nursery struggle far away. And it seemed that the night, so sharp and still, the physical world, would wait motionless until they all came back.

You've lost, Breavman addressed them out loud. It's a hypnotists' tournament, this little life of ours, and I'm the winner.

He decided to share the prize with Krantz.

The screen in the window above Krantz's bed had a bulge in it. When Breavman tapped it from the outside it created a miniature thunder.

His face did not appear. Breavman tapped again. Krantz's disembodied voice began in a monotone.

"You are stepping on the flowers, Breavman. If you look down, you will discover that you are in a flower-bed. Why are you standing on the flowers, Breavman?"

"Krantz, listen to this: The last refuge of the insomniac is a sense of superiority to the sleeping world."

"That's very good, Breavman. Good night."

"The last superiority of the refuge is a sleeping sense of the insomniac world."

"Oh, excellent."

"The refuge world of the superiority is a last sense of the sleeping insomniac."

"Umm. Yes."

There was a creaking of springs and Krantz blinked out of the window.

"Hello, Breavman."

"You can go back to sleep now, Krantz. I just wanted to wake you up."

"Well, you might as well rouse the camp. Rouse the camp, Breavman! It's the night."

"For what?"

"A Children's Crusade. We'll march on Montreal."

"So there's a reason for all this discipline. Forgive me, Krantz, I should have known."

They planned the assault on Montreal and the ensuing martyrdom with sinister enthusiasm. After four minutes of talk Breavman broke into the fantasy.

"Is this for my benefit, Krantz? Some sort of charitable therapy?"

"God damn you, Breavman!"

The bed creaked again and in a few seconds Krantz was outside, wearing a bathrobe and a towel around his neck.

"Let's walk, Breavman."

"You were humouring me, Krantz."

"I don't know how you can be so perceptive in one instant and so miserably blind in another. I admit it. I was asleep and I felt like telling you to fuck off. Besides, Anne was in bed with me."

"I'm sorry, I –"

"No, I want to talk to you, now. I've been trying to get to talk to you for weeks."

"What?"

"You've made yourself completely unavailable, Breavman. To me, to everyone. . . ."

They stood beside the canoe racks, talking, listening to the water. The sand was damp and it was really too cold to be there but neither wished to cripple the communication that had begun, and which both knew was fragile.

The mist along the shore began to weave itself thick out of snaky wisps, and the edge of the sky brightened into a royal blue.

They told each other about their girls, a little solemnly, carefully omitting any sexual information.

13

He watched Martin clean his nose, his great Caesarian nose that should have sponsored historic campaigns but only counted grass and pine needles.

Every morning Martin got up half an hour early to fulfil the ritual.

Toothpicks, cotton-wool, vaseline, mirrors.

Breavman asked him why.

"I like to have a clean nose."

Martin asked Breavman to mail a letter to his brother. Mrs. Stark had given instructions that they be intercepted and destroyed. Breavman read them and they brought him closer to the boy's anguish.

> Dear Bully fat Bully you dirty
>
> I got your last thirty-four letters and saw in a second the millions of lies. I hope you starve and your boner breaks in half with lots of screams and lets the beetles out after what you told her about me. Why don't you fill your mouth with towels and razor-blades. Mummy is not a stupid skull she sneaked a look in the flashlight and read the poison shit you wrote me under the blankets.
>
> love your brother,
> MARTIN STARK

14

Day off. Despite the hot drive in the bus he was exhilarated to be back in Montreal. But who were the bastards responsible for tearing down the best parts of the city?

He visited his mother, was unable to make her understand he'd been away. Same horror as always.

He walked along Sherbrooke Street. The women of Montreal were beautiful. Launched from tiny ankles, their legs shot up like guided missiles into atmospheres of private height.

He formed wild theories out of pleats and creases.

Wrists, white and fast as falling stars, plunged him into armholes. Tonight they would have to comb his eyeballs out of all their hair.

He planted hundreds of hands in bosoms, like hidden money.

Therefore he called on Tamara.

"Come in, old chappie, old."

Smell of turpentine. Another batch of agonized self-portraits.

"Tamara, you're the only woman I can talk to. For the past two weeks I've gone to sleep with your mouth in my hand."

"How's camp? How's Krantz?"

"Flourishing. But he'll never make a Compassionate P."

"You smell delicious. And you're so brown. Yummy."

"Let's be immoderate."

"Good idea in any given situation."

"Let's praise each other's genitalia. Don't you hate that word?"

"For women. It's good for men. Sounds loopy – things hanging. Makes me think of chandelier."

"You're great, Tamara. God, I like being with you. I can be anything."

"So can I."

And Shell with her open gift, it struck him, forced him into a kind of nobility.

"Let's resort to everything."

They left the room at five in the morning to eat a huge meal at the China Gardens. Laughing like maniacs, they fed each other with chopsticks and decided they were in love. The waiters stared. They hadn't bothered to remove the paint.

Walking back, they talked about Shell, how beautiful she was. He asked Tamara if she would mind his phoning New York.

"Of course not. She's something else."

Shell was sleepy but glad to hear from him. She spoke in a little girl's voice. He told her he loved her.

He took the early morning bus back to camp. Immortal Tamara, she walked with him to the terminal. After one hour's sleep he called that real affection.

15

Now we must take a closer look at Breavman's journal:

Friday night. Sabbath. Ritual music on the PA. Holy, holy, holy, Lord God of Hosts. The earth is full of your glory. If I could only end my hate. If I could believe what they wrote and wrapped in silk and crowned with gold. I want to write the word.

All our bodies are brown. All the children are dressed in white. Make us able to worship.

Take me home again. Build up my house again. Make me a dweller in thee. Take my pain. I can't use it any longer. It makes nothing beautiful. It makes the leaves into cinders. It makes the water foul. It makes your body into a stone. Holy life. Let me lead it. I don't want to hate. Let me flourish. Let the dream of you flourish in me.

Brother, give me your new car. I want to ride to my love. In return I offer you this wheelchair. Brother, give me all your money. I want to buy everything my love wants. In return I offer you blindness so you may live the rest of your days in absolute control over everyone. Brother, give me your wife. It is she whom I love. In return I have commanded all the whores of the city to give you infinite credit.

Thou. Help me to work. All the works of my hand belong to you. Do not let me make my offering so paltry. Do not make me insane. Do not let me descend raving your name.

I have no taste for flesh but my own.

Lead me away from safety. There is no safety where I am.

How shall I dedicate my days to thee? Now I have finally said it. How shall I dedicate my days to thee?

16

Dearest Shell,

Your jade earring with the filigree silver. I pictured it on your ear. Then I pictured the side of your head and the wind-paths of hair. Then your face. Finally all your beauty.

Then I remembered your suspicion of beauty's praise, so I praised your soul, yours being the only one I believe in.

I discovered that the beauty of your eyes and flesh was just the soul's everyday clothes. It turned to music when I asked it what it wore on Sabbath.

All my love, darling,

LAWRENCE

17

Anne and Breavman were on night duty together. They sat on the steps of one of the bunks waiting for the counsellors to check in.

Yes, yes, Krantz was in the city on camp business.

Her braid was like a thick twisting river. Fireflies, some as high as the tops of the pines, some beside the roots.

Here is my poem for you.

> I don't know you, Anne.
> I don't know you, Anne.
> I don't know you, Anne.

Eternal theme: small flies and moths flinging themselves against the light bulb.

"This is the kind of night I'd like to get drunk," she said.

"I'd like to get sober."

A light rain began to fall. He turned up his face, trying to give himself away.

"I'm going for a walk."

"May I come along? I don't mind asking because I feel I know you. Krantz has told me so much."

It rained for ten seconds. They walked down the road to the village. They stopped where the pine scent was heaviest. He found himself swaying back and forth as though he were in a synagogue. He wanted her, and the more he wanted her the more he became a part of the mist and trees. I'll never get out of this, he told himself. This is where I'll stay. I like the smell. I like being that close, that far away. He felt he was manufacturing the mist. It was steaming out of his pores.

"I'll go back if you want to stay alone."

He didn't answer for a thousand years.

"No, we both better go."

He didn't move.

"What's that?" Anne asked about a noise.

He began to tell her about swallows, cliff-dwelling swallows, barn-dwelling swallows. He knew everything about swallows. He had disguised himself as a swallow and lived among them to learn their ways.

He was standing close to her but he received no trace of the radar signal to embrace. He walked swiftly away. He came back. He pulled her braid. It was thick, as he imagined. He strode away again and snatched a stick from the bushes by the side of the road.

He swung it wildly, smashing the foliage. He beat the ground around her feet. She danced, laughing. He raised the dust knee-high. But the bushes had to be attacked again, the trunks of the trees, the low yellow grass, white in the night. Then more dust, the branch nicking her ankles. He wanted to raise the dust over both of them, slice up their bodies with the sharp switch.

She ran from him. He ran behind her, whipping the calves of her legs. They were both screaming with laughter. She ran to the lights of the camp.

18

> Dear Anne
> I'd like
> to watch
> your toes
> when you're
> naked.

Which he delivered to her several hundred times with his eyes without even thinking.

19

"Fifty cents for a hand on her crotch."

Krantz was joking with Breavman about selling Anne to him piece by piece. Breavman didn't like the joke but he laughed.

"An almost unused nipple for three bits?"

Oh, Krantz.

They had quarrelled over Breavman's treatment of Martin. Breavman had categorically refused to enjoin the boy to participate in group activities. He had put his job on the line.

"You know we can't start looking for replacements at this point in the season."

"In that case you'll have to let me handle him my own way."

"I'm not telling you to force him into activities, but I swear you encourage him in the other direction."

"I enjoy his madness. He enjoys his madness. He's the only free person I've ever met. Nothing that anybody else does is as important as what he does."

"You're talking a lot of nonsense, Breavman."

"Probably."

Then Breavman had decided he couldn't deliver a sermon to the camp on Saturday morning when his turn came around. He had nothing to say to anyone.

Krantz looked at him squarely.

"You made a mistake, coming up here, didn't you?"

"And you made one asking me. We both wanted to prove different things. So now you know you're your own man, Krantz."

"Yes," he said slowly. "I know."

It was a moment, this true meeting, and Breavman didn't try to stretch it into a guarantee. He had trained himself to delight in the fraction. "What thou lovest well remains, the rest is dross."

"Of course you know that you're identifying with Martin and are only excluding yourself when you allow him to separate himself from the group."

"Not that jargon, Krantz, please."

"I remember everything, Breavman. But I can't live in it."

"Good."

Therefore Breavman was obliged to laugh when Anne joined them and Krantz said, "Buttocks are going very cheap."

20

In the evening he stayed motionless on the mess hall balcony. Krantz was about to put a record on the PA.

"Hey, Anne, you want Mozart, the Forty-ninth?" he shouted. She ran towards him.

Breavman saw clover in the grass, a discovery, and mist drifting across the tops of the low mountains, like the fade in a photo. Ripples on the water moving in the same direction as the mist, from black into silver into black.

He didn't move a muscle, didn't know whether he was at peace or paralysed.

Steve, the Hungarian tractor driver, passed below the balcony, picking a white flower from a bush. They were levelling out some land for another playing field, filling in a marsh.

The flute-bird had a needle in its whistle. A broken door down the hill beside the thick-bottomed pines.

> *"London Bridge is falling down*
> *falling down*
> *falling down"*

sang a file of children.

Down the pine-needled path stood Martin, motionless as Breavman, his arm stretched out in a Fascist salute, his sleeve rolled up.

He was waiting for mosquitoes to land.

Martin had a new obsession. He elected himself to be the Scourge of Mosquitoes, counting them as he killed them. There was nothing frantic about his technique. He extended his arm and invited them. When one landed, wham! up came the other hand. "I hate you," he told each one individually, and noted the statistic.

Martin saw his counsellor standing on the balcony.

"A hundred and eighty," he called up as greeting.

Mozart came loud over the PA, sewing together everything that Breavman observed. It wove, it married the two figures bending over the records, whatever the music touched, child trapped in London Bridge, mountain-top dissolving in mist, empty swing rocking like a pendulum, the row of glistening red canoes, the players clustered underneath the basket, leaping for the ball like a stroboscopic photo of a splashing drop of water – whatever it touched was frozen in an immense tapestry. He was in it, a figure by a railing.

21

Since his mission against the mosquitoes had begun, Martin's enjoyment percentages soared. All the days were up around 98 per cent. The other boys delighted in him and made him the ornament of the bunk, to be shown off to visitors and wondered at. Martin remained an innocent performer. He spent most afternoons down at the marsh where the tractors were preparing new fields to run on. His arm was swollen with bites. Breavman applied calamine.

On his next day off Breavman took a canoe down the lake. Red-wing blackbirds rose and plunged into the reeds. He ripped open a stalk of a waterlily. It was veined with purple foam.

The lake was glass-calm. He could make out sounds of camp from time to time, the PA announcing General Swim; recorded music filtered through the forest and crept over the water.

He went down the creek as far as he could before sandbars

stopped him. The only indication of current was the leaning underwater weeds. Clams black and thickly coated with mud – an unclean food. A snap of water and the green stretched-out body of a frog zoomed under the canoe. The low sun was blinding. As he paddled back to his camp-site it turned the paddle gold.

He built a fire, spread out his sleeping bag in the moss, and prepared to watch the sky.

The sun is always part of the sky, but the moon is a splendid and remote stranger. The moon. Your eye keeps coming back to it as it would do to a beautiful woman in a restaurant. He thought about Shell. The same moment he believed he had the confidence to live alone he believed he could live with Shell.

The mist was riding slowly on the reflection of birch trees; now it was piled like a snowdrift.

Four hours later he awakened with a start and grabbed his axe.

"It's Martin Stark," said Martin.

The fire was still giving some light, but not enough. He shone his flash in the boy's face. One cheek had been badly scratched by branches but the boy grinned widely.

"What's your favourite store?"

"What are you doing out here in the middle of the night?"

"What's your favourite store?"

Breavman wrapped the sleeping bag around the boy and ruffled his hair.

"Dionne's."

"What's your favourite parking lot?"

"Dionne's Parking Lot."

When the ritual was finished Breavman packed up, lifted him into the canoe, and shoved off for camp. He didn't want to think about what would have happened if Martin hadn't been able to find him. That cheek needed iodine. And it seemed that some of the bites were infected.

It was beautiful paddling back, reeds scraping the bottom of the canoe and turning it into a big fragile drum. Martin was an Indian chief squatting beside him, bundled in the sleeping bag. The sky displayed continents of fire.

"When I'm back home," Martin said loudly, "rats eat me."

"I'm sorry, Martin."

"Hundreds and hundreds of them."

When Breavman saw the lights of the camp he had a wild urge to pass them, to keep paddling up the lake with the boy, make a site somewhere up the shore among the naked birch trees.

"Keep it down, Martin. They'll kill us if they hear us."

"That would be all right."

22

Green? Beige? Riding in the bus he tried to remember the colour of his mother's room. In this way he avoided thinking about her lying there. Some careful shade determined at a medical conference.

In this room she spends her time. It has a good view of the southern slopes of Mount Royal. In the spring you get the smell of lilacs. You want to throw the window open to get more of the perfume, but you can't. The window slides up only so far. They don't want any suicides littering the lawn.

"We haven't seen you for a while, Mr. Breavman," said the head nurse.

"Haven't we?"

His mother was staring at the ceiling. He looked up there himself. Maybe something was going on that nobody knew about.

The walls were clever grey.

"Are you feeling better, Mother?" He gave the cue.

"Am I feeling better? better for what? that I should go out-side and see what he's doing with his life? thank you, for that I don't have to go outside, for that I can lie here, in this room beside the crazy people, your mother in an insane asylum. . . .

"You know it isn't that, Mother. Just somewhere you can rest—"

"Rest! How can I rest with what I know? traitor for a son, don't you think I know where I am? with their needles and their polite manner, a mother like this and he's away swimming—"

"But, Mother, nobody's trying to hurt—"

What was he doing, trying to argue with her? She flung out one arm and groped for something on the night table, but everything had been taken away.

"Don't interrupt your mother, haven't I suffered enough? a sick man for fifteen years, don't I know? don't I know, don't *know* . . . ?"

"Mother, please, don't scream—"

"Oh! he's ashamed of his mother, his mother will wake up the neighbours, his mother will frighten away his goyish girlfriends, traitor! what all of you have done to me! a mother has to be quiet, I was beautiful, I came from Russia a beauty, people looked at me—"

"Let me speak to you—"

"People spoke to me, does my child speak to me? the world knows I lie here like a stone, a beauty, they called me a Russian beauty, but what I gave to my child, to treat a mother, I can't stand to think of it, you should have it from your own child like today is Tuesday over the whole world you should have it from your child what I had, rat in my house, I can't believe my life, that this should happen to me, I was so good to my parents, my mother had cancer, the doctor held her stomach in his hand, does anyone try to help me? does my son lift a finger? Cancer! cancer! I had to see everything, I had to give my life away to sick people, this isn't my life, to see these things, your father would kill you, my face is old, I don't know who I am in the mirror, wrinkles where I was beautiful. . . ."

He sat back, didn't try to break in again. If she let him speak she wouldn't hear. He really didn't know what he would have been able to say had he known she was listening.

He attempted to let his mind wander, but he hung on every wild detail, waiting for the hour to be up.

He knocked on Tamara's door at about ten o'clock. There were a few whispers exchanged inside. She called out, "Who is it?"

"Breavman from the north. But you're busy."

"Yes."

"Okay. Night."

"Night."

Good night, Tamara. It's all right to share your mouth. It belongs to everyone, like a park.

He wrote two letters to Shell and then phoned her so he could get to sleep.

23

Ed's bunk was expected to win the baseball game.

The foul-lines were marked with Israeli flags.

What right did he have to resent their using the symbol? It wasn't engraved on his shield.

A child brandished a Pepsi, cheering for his side.

Breavman passed out hot dogs. He was glad he'd learned to suspect his Gentile neighbours of uncleanliness, not to believe in flags. Now he could apply that training to his own tribe.

A home run.

Send your children to the academies in Alexandria. Don't be surprised if they come back Alexandrians.

Three cheers. Mazel tov.

Hello Canada, you big Canada, you dull, beautiful resources. Everybody is Canadian. The Jew's disguise won't work.

When it was Ed's turn to umpire, Breavman walked across the field to the marsh and watched Martin kill mosquitoes. The tractor man knew him well because he often came to see Martin fulfil his mission.

The boy had killed over six thousand mosquitoes.

"I'll kill some for you, Martin."

"That won't help my score."

"Then I'll start my own score."

"I'll beat you."

Martin's feet were wet. Some of the bites were definitely infected. He should send him back to the bunk, but he seemed to be enjoying himself so thoroughly. All his days were 99 per cent.

"I dare you to start your own score."

As they accompanied their groups back to the camp Ed said, "Not only did you lose the game, Breavman, but you owe me five dollars."

"What for?"

"Wanda. Last night."

"Oh, God, the pool. I'd forgotten."

He checked his journal and gratefully paid the money.

24

All the days were sunny and the bodies bronze. All he watched was the sand and the exposed flesh, marvelling at the softer city white when a strap fell away. He wanted all the strange flesh-shadows.

He hardly ever looked at the sky. A bird swooping low over the beach surprised him. One of the Brandenburgs was blaring over the PA. He was lying on his back, eyes closed, annihilating himself in the heat and glare and music. Suddenly someone was kneeling over him.

"Let me squeeze it," went Anne's voice.

He opened his eyes and shivered.

"No, let me," Wanda laughed.

They were trying to get at a blackhead in his forehead.

"Leave me alone," he shouted like a maniac.

The violence of his reaction astonished them.

He pretended to smile, waited a decent interval, left the beach. The bunk was too cool. The night air hadn't been cooked away. He looked around the small wooden cubicle. His laundry bag was bulging. He'd forgotten to send it off. That couldn't be right. Not right for him. There was a box of Ritz crackers on the window-sill. That wasn't how he was supposed to eat. He pulled out his journal. That wasn't how he was supposed to write.

25

Martin Stark was killed in the first week of August 1958. He was accidentally run over by a bulldozer which was clearing a marshy area. The driver of the bulldozer, the Hungarian named Steve, was not aware that he had hit anything except the usual clumps, roots, stones. Martin was probably hiding in the reeds the better to trap his enemy.

When he didn't show for supper Breavman thought he might be up there. He asked a junior counsellor to sit at his table. He walked leisurely to the marsh, glad for an excuse to leave the noisy mess hall.

He heard a noise from the weeds. He imagined that Martin had seen him coming and wanted to play a hiding game. He took off his shoes and waded in. He was terribly squashed, a tractor tread right across his back. He was lying face down. When Breavman turned him over his mouth was full of guts.

Breavman walked back to the mess hall and told Krantz.

His face went white. They agreed that the campers must not find out and that the body be removed secretly. Krantz went up to the marsh and returned in a few minutes.

"You stay up there until the camp's asleep. Ed will take your bunk."

"I want to go into town with the body," Breavman said.

"We'll see."

"No, we won't see. I'm going in with Martin."

"Breavman, get the hell up there now and don't give me arguments at a time like this. What's the matter with you?"

He stood guard for a few hours. Nobody came by. The mosquitoes were very bad. He wondered what they were doing to the body. They'd been all over when he found it. There wasn't much of a moon. He could hear the seniors singing at their bonfire. At about one in the morning the police and ambulance arrived. They worked under the headlights.

"I'm going in with him."

Krantz had just spoken to Mrs. Stark on the phone. She had been remarkably calm. She had even mentioned that she wouldn't press charges of criminal negligence. Krantz was very shaken.

"All right."

"And I'm not coming back."

"What do you mean you're not coming back? Don't start with me now, Breavman."

"I'm quitting."

"Camp runs another three weeks. I don't have anybody to replace you."

"I don't care."

Krantz grabbed his arm.

"You got a contract, Breavman."

"Screw the contract. Don't pay me."

"You phony little bastard, at a time like this –"

"And you owe me five dollars. I had Wanda first. July eleventh, if you want to see my journal."

"For Christ's sake, Breavman, what are you talking about? What are you talking about? Don't you see where you are? Don't you see what is happening? A child has been killed and you're talking about a lay –"

"A lay. That's your language. Five dollars, Krantz. Then I'm getting out of here. This isn't where I'm supposed to be –"

It was impossible to say who threw the first punch.

26

DON'T SQUEEZE ANYTHING OUT OF THE BODY IT DOESN'T OWE YOU ANYTHING was the complete entry.

He banged it out on the bus to Montreal, typewriter on knees.

It was the worst stretch of the road, signs and gas stations, and the back of the driver's neck, and his damn washable plastic shirt was boiling him.

If only death could seize him, come through the scum, dignify.

What was it they sang at the end of the book?

Strength! strength! let us renew ourselves!

He would never learn the names of the trees he passed, he'd never learn anything, he'd always confront a lazy mystery. He wanted to be the tall black mourner who learns everything at the hole.

I'm sorry, Father, I don't know the Latin for butterflies, I don't know what stone the lookout is made of.

The driver was having trouble with the doors. Maybe they'd never open. How would it be to suffocate in a plastic shirt?

27

Dearest Shell,

It will take me a little while to tell you.

It's two in the morning. You're sleeping between the green-striped sheets we bought together and I know exactly how your body looks. You are lying on your side, knees bent like a jockey, and you've probably pushed the pillow off the bed and your hair looks like calligraphy, and one hand is cupped beside your mouth, and one arm leads over the edge like a bowsprit and your fingers are limp like things that are drifting.

It's wonderful to be able to speak to you, my darling Shell. I can be peaceful because I know what I want to say.

I'm afraid of loneliness. Just visit a mental hospital or factory, sit in a bus or cafeteria. Everywhere people are living in utter loneliness. I tremble when I think of all the single voices raised, lottery-chance hooks aimed at the sky. And their bodies are growing old, hearts beginning to leak like old accordions, trouble in the kidneys, sphincters going limp like old elastic bands. It's happening to us, to you under the green stripes. It makes me want to take your hand. And this is the miracle that all the juke-boxes are eating quarters for. That we can protest this indifferent massacre. Taking your hand is a very good protest. I wish you were beside me now.

I went to a funeral today. It was no way to bury a child. His real death contrasted violently with the hush-hush sacredness of the chapel. The beautiful words didn't belong on the rabbi's lips. I don't know if any modern man is fit to bury a person. The family's grief was real, but the air-conditioned chapel conspired against its expression. I felt lousy and choked because I had nothing to say to the corpse. When they carried away the undersized coffin I thought the boy was cheated.

I can't claim any lesson. When you read my journal you'll see how close I am to murder. I can't even think about it or I stop moving. I mean literally. I can't move a muscle. All I know is that something prosaic, the comfortable world, has been destroyed irrevocably, and something important guaranteed.

A religious stink hovers above this city and we all breathe it. Work goes on at the Oratoire St. Joseph, the copper dome is raised. The Temple Emmanuel initiates a building fund. A religious stink composed of musty shrine and tabernacle smells, decayed wreaths and rotting bar-mitzvah tables. Boredom, money, vanity, guilt, packs the pews. The candles, memorials, eternal lights shine unconvincingly, like neon signs, sincere as advertising. The holy vessels belch miasmal smoke. Good lovers turn away.

I'm not a good lover or I'd be with you now. I'd be beside you, not using this longing for a proof of feeling. That's why I'm writing you and sending you this summer's journal. I want you to know something about me. Here it is day by day. Dearest Shell, if you let me I'd always keep you four hundred miles away and write you pretty poems and letters. That's true. I'm afraid to live any place but in expectation. I'm no life-risk.

At the beginning of the summer we said: let's be surgical. I don't want to see or hear from you. I'd like to counterpoint this with tenderness but I'm not going to. I want no attachments. I want to begin again. I think I love you, but I love the idea of a clean slate more. I can say these things to you because we've come that close. The temptation of discipline makes me ruthless.

I want to end this letter now. It's the first one I didn't make a carbon of. I'm close to flying down and jumping into bed beside you. Please don't phone or write. Something wants to begin in me.

LAWRENCE

Shell sent three telegrams that he didn't answer. Five times he allowed his phone to ring all night.

One morning she awakened suddenly and couldn't catch her breath. Lawrence had done exactly the same thing to her as Gordon – the letters, everything!

28

They drank patiently, waiting for incoherence.

"You know, of course, Tamara, that we're losing the Cold War?"

"No!"

"Plain as the nose. You know what Chinese youth are doing this very minute?"

"Smelting pig-iron in back yards?"

"Correct. And the Russians are learning trigonometry in kindergarten. What do you think about that, Tamara?"

"Black thoughts."

"But it doesn't matter, Tamara."

"Why?"

He was trying to stand a bottle on its pouring rim.

"I'll tell you why, Tamara. Because we're all ripe for a concentration camp."

That was a little brutal for their stage of intoxication. On the couch he mumbled beside her.

"What are you saying?"

"I'm not saying anything."

"You were saying something."

"Do you want to know what I'm saying, Tamara?"

"Yeah."

"You really want to know?"

"Yes."

"All right, I'll tell you."

Silence.

"Well?"

"I'll tell you."

"Okay, you tell me."

"I'm saying this: . . ."

There was a pause. He leaped up, ran to the window, smashed his fist through the glass.

"Get the car, Krantz," he screamed. *"Get the car, get the car! . . ."*

29

Let us study one more shadow.

He was heading towards Côte des Neiges. Patricia was sleeping back at his room on Stanley, profound sleep of isolation, her red hair fallen on her shoulders as if arranged by a Botticelli wind.

He could not help thinking that she was too beautiful for him to have, that he wasn't tall enough or straight, that people didn't turn to look at him in street-cars, that he didn't command the glory of the flesh.

She deserved someone, an athlete perhaps, who moved with a grace equal to hers, exercised the same immediate tyranny of beauty in face and limb.

He met her at a cast party. She had played the lead in *Hedda Gabler*. A cold bitch, she'd done it well, all the ambition and vine leaves. She was as beautiful as Shell, Tamara, one of the great. She was from Winnipeg.

"Do they have Art in Winnipeg?"

Later on that night they walked up Mountain Street. Breavman showed her an iron fence which hid in its calligraphy silhouettes of swallows, rabbits, chipmunks. She opened fast to him. She told him she had an ulcer. Christ, at her age.

"How old are you?"

"Eighteen. I know you're surprised."

"I'm surprised you can be that calm and live with whatever it is that's eating your stomach."

But something had to pay for the way she moved, her steps like early Spanish music, her face which acted above pain.

He showed her curious parts of the city that night. He tried to see his eighteen-year-old city again. Here was a wall he had loved. There was a crazy filigree doorway he wanted her to see, but when they approached he saw the building had been torn down.

"Où sont les neiges?" he said theatrically.

She looked straight at him and said, "You've won me, Lawrence Breavman."

And he supposed that that was what he had been trying to do.

They lay apart like two slabs. Nothing his hands or mouth could do involved him in her beauty. It was like years ago with Tamara, the silent torture bed.

He knew he couldn't begin the whole process again. What had happened to his plan? They finally found words to say and tenderness, the kind that follows failure.

They stayed in the room together.

By the end of the next day he had written a still-born poem about two armies marching to battle from different corners of a continent. They never meet in conflict in the central plain. Winter eats through the battalions like a storm of moths at a brocade gown, leaving the metal threads of artillery strewn gunnerless miles behind the frozen men, pointless designs on a vast closet floor. Then months later two corporals of different language meet in a green, unblasted field. Their feet are bound with strips of cloth torn from the uniforms of superiors. The field they meet on is the one that distant powerful marshals ordained for glory. Because the men have come from different directions they face each other, but they have forgotten why they stumbled there.

That next night he watched her move about his room. He had never seen anything so beautiful. She was nested in a brown chair studying a script. He remembered a colour he loved in the crucible of melted brass. Her hair was that colour and her warm body seemed to reflect it just as the caster's face glows above the poured moulds.

> PAUVRE GRANDE BEAUTÉ!
> POOR PERFECT BEAUTY!

He gave all his silent praise for her limbs, lips, not to the clamour of personal desire, but to the pure demand of excellence.

They had talked enough for her to be naked. The line of her belly reminded him of the soft forms drawn on the cave wall by the artist-hunter. He remembered her intestines.

> QUEL MAL MYSTÉRIEUX RONGE SON FLANC
> D'ATHLÈTE?
> WHAT UNKNOWN EVIL HARROWS HER LITHE
> SIDE?

Lying beside her he thought wildly that a miracle would deliver them into a sexual embrace. He didn't know why, because they were nice people, the natural language of bodies, because she was leaving tomorrow. She rested her hand on his thigh, no desire in the touch. She went to sleep and he opened his eyes in the black and his room was never emptier or a woman further away. He listened to her breathing. It was like the delicate engine of some cruel machine spreading distance after distance between them. Her sleep was the final withdrawal, more perfect than anything she could say or do. She slept with a deeper grace than that with which she moved.

He knew that hair couldn't feel; he kissed her hair.

He was heading towards Côte des Neiges. The night had been devised by a purist of Montreal autumns. A light rain made the black iron fences shine. Leaves lay precisely etched on the wet pavement, flat as if they'd fallen from diaries. A wind blurred the leaves of the young acacia on MacGregor Street. He was walking an old route of fences and mansions he knew by heart.

The need for Shell stabbed him in a few seconds. He actually felt himself impaled in the air by a spear of longing. And with the longing came a burden of loneliness he knew he could not support. Why were they in different cities?

He ran to the Mount Royal Hotel. A cleaning lady on her knees thanked him for the mud.

He was dialling, shouting at the operator, reversing the charges.

The phone rang nine times before she answered it.

"Shell!"

"I wasn't going to answer."

"Marry me! That's what I want."

There was a long silence.

"Lawrence, you can't treat people like this."

"Won't you marry me?"

"I read your journal."

Oh, her voice was so beautiful, fuzzy with sleep.

"Never mind my journal. I know I hurt you. Please don't remember it."

"I want to go back to sleep."

"Don't hang up."

"I won't hang up," she said wearily. "I'll wait till you say good-bye."

"I love you, Shell."

There was another long silence and he thought he heard her crying.

"I do. Really."

"Please go away. I can't be what you need."

"Yes, you can. You are."

"Nobody can be what you need."

"Shell, this is crazy, talking this way, four hundred miles apart. I'm coming to New York."

"Have you any money?"

"What kind of a question is that?"

"Do you have any money for a ticket? You quit camp, and I know you didn't have much when you started."

He never heard her voice so bitter. It sobered him.

"I'm coming."

"Because I don't want to wait for you if you're not."

"Shell?"

"Yes."

"Is there anything left?"

"I don't know."

"We'll talk."

"All right. I'll say good night now."

She said that in her old voice, the voice that accepted him and helped him with his ambitions. It made him sad to hear it. For himself, he had exhausted the emotion that impelled the call. He didn't need to go to New York.

30

He began his tour through the heart streets of Montreal. The streets were changing. The Victorian gingerbread was going down everywhere, and on every second corner was the half-covered skeleton of a new, flat office building. The city seemed fierce to go modern, as though it had suddenly been converted to some new theory of hygiene and had learned with horror that it was impossible to scrape the dirt out of gargoyle crevices and carved grape vines, and therefore was determined to cauterize the whole landscape.

But they were beautiful. They were the only beauty, the last magic. Breavman knew what he knew, that their bodies never died. Everything else was fiction. It was the beauty they carried. He remembered them all, there was nothing lost. To serve them. His mind sang praise as he climbed a street to the mountain.

For the body of Heather, which slept and slept.

For the body of Bertha, which fell with apples and a flute.

For the body of Lisa, early and late, which smelled of speed and forests.

For the body of Tamara, whose thighs made him a fetishist of thighs.

For the body of Norma, goose-fleshed, wet.

For the body of Patricia, which he had still to tame.

For the body of Shell, which was altogether sweet in his memory, which he loved as he walked, the little breasts he wrote about, and her hair which was so black it shone blue.

For all the bodies in and out of bathing suits, clothes, water, going between rooms, lying on grass, taking the print of grass, dancing discipline, leaping over horses, growing in mirrors, felt like treasure, slobbered over, cheated for, all of them, the great ballet line, the cream in them, the sun on them, the oil anointed.

A thousand shadows, a single fire, everything that happened, twisted by telling, served the vision, and when he saw it, he was in the very centre of things.

Blindly he climbed the wooden steps that led up the side of the mountain. He was stopped by the high walls of the hospital. Its Italian towers looked sinister. His mother was sleeping in one of them.

He turned and looked at the city below him.

The heart of the city wasn't down there among the new

buildings and widened streets. It was right over there at the Allan, which, with drugs and electricity, was keeping the businessmen sane and their wives from suicide and their children free from hatred. The hospital was the true heart, pumping stability and erections and orgasms and sleep into all the withering commercial limbs. His mother was sleeping in one of the towers. With windows that didn't quite open.

The restaurant bathed the corner of Stanley and St. Catherine in a light that made your skin yellow and the veins show through. It was a big place, mirrored, crowded as usual. There wasn't a woman he could see. Breavman noted that a lot of the men used hair tonic; the sides of their heads seemed shiny and wet. Most of them were thin. And there seemed to be a uniform, almost. Tight chinos with belts in the back, V-neck sweaters without shirts.

He sat at a table. He was very thirsty. He felt in his pocket. Shell was right. He didn't have much money.

No, he wouldn't go to New York. He knew that. But he must always be connected to her. That must never be severed. Everything was simple as long as he was connected to her, as long as they remembered.

One day what he did to her, to the child, would enter his understanding with such a smash of guilt that he would sit motionless for days, until others carried him and medical machines brought him back to speech.

But that was not today.

The juke-box wailed. He believed he understood the longing of the cheap tunes better than anyone there. The Wurlitzer was a great beast, blinking in pain. It was everybody's neon wound. A suffering ventriloquist. It was the kind of pet people wanted. An eternal bear for baiting, with electric blood. Breavman had a quarter to spare. It was fat, it loved its chains, it gobbled and was ready to fester all night.

Breavman thought he'd just sit back and sip his Orange

Crush. A memory hit him urgently and he asked a waitress for her pencil. On a napkin he scribbled:

> Jesus! I just remembered what Lisa's favourite game was. After a heavy snow we would go into a back yard with a few of our friends. The expanse of snow would be white and unbroken. Bertha was the spinner. You held her hands while she turned on her heels, you circled her until your feet left the ground. Then she let go and you flew over the snow. You remained still in whatever position you landed. When everyone had been flung in this fashion into the fresh snow, the beautiful part of the game began. You stood up carefully, taking great pains not to disturb the impression you had made. Now the comparisons. Of course you would have done your best to land in some crazy position, arms and legs sticking out. Then we walked away, leaving a lovely white field of blossom-like shapes with footprint stems.

Afterword

BY PAUL QUARRINGTON

The Favourite Game was published in the fall of 1963.

That year seems wintry in retrospect, the tragedy of President Kennedy's assassination setting the tone. There were noteworthy exits in the literary world: Jean Cocteau, Robert Frost, Aldous Huxley, Clifford Odets, William Carlos Williams. And it was the year a silence began: *Raise High the Roof Beams, Carpenters* and *Seymour: An Introduction* remains J. D. Salinger's last published book.

But, to echo Bob Dylan, the times they were a-changin'. In Liverpool four young musicians who called themselves the Beatles were preparing to change things, absolutely and forever. Also living in England at that time was a young poet from Montreal. Leonard Cohen made an audacious entrance as a novelist with *The Favourite Game*. Consider the dust-jacket copy to the first edition. Cohen writes:

I was born in Montreal in 1934. I studied at McGill and Columbia Universities. Lived in London as a Lord, pursuing the fair, my accent opening the tightest Georgian palaces where I flourished dark and magnificent as Othello. In Oslo where I existed in a Nazi poster. In Cuba, the only tourist in Havana, perhaps in the world, where I destroyed my beard on the shores of Veradere, burnt it in nostalgia and anger for the Fidel I used to know. In Greece, where my gothic insincerities were purged and my style purified under the influence of empty mountains and a foreign mate who cherished simple English. In Montreal, where I always return, scene of the steep streets which support the romantic academies of Canadian Poesy in which I was trained, seat of my family, old as the Indians, more powerful than the Elders of Zion, the last merchants to take blood seriously. I accept money from governments, women, poem sales, and if forced, from employers. I have no hobbies.

Opening the book's cover, the reader encounters more of this unbridled spirit. *The Favourite Game* is a morally brave book, intimate and unflinching. From the first page, the author reveals himself to be unusual in his concerns and methods. "It is easy to display a wound, the proud scars of combat," he announces. "It is hard to show a pimple."

I do not mean to imply that the world had never seen anything like *The Favourite Game.* The book falls neatly into a literary category and tradition. It is a *bildungsroman*, which is translated from the German exactly as "formation novel" or, more expressively, "education novel." The term refers to a novel which represents a person's formative years; Charles Dickens's *David Copperfield* springs to mind as an example.

There is always a temptation to read such books as autobiography. Certainly correlations can be established between the fiction and what we know of Cohen's life. The fifth chapter of the opening book deals with the prominence of the Montreal-based Breavman family, and the most cursory investigation reveals that Cohen emerged from the same sort of background. Many of the poems in the novel are taken from

Cohen's *The Spice-Box of Earth*, further blurring any distinction between Lawrence Breavman and his creator.

The Favourite Game, again like *David Copperfield*, falls into a subset of the *bildungsroman*, the *künstlerroman*, a novel which portrays the maturation of an artist (in German, *ein künstler*). In presenting an intimate portrait of the poet, Cohen may well have incorporated some aspects of his own life, but his concerns are broad, and have to do with the complicated interplay between beauty, quotidian existence, and the human spirit. Although we should not seek factual, historical connections between the author and his literary surrogate, we may perhaps safely assume an emotional or spiritual one. Such novels, at least the best of them, have a compelling intensity. They resonate with a true heartfelt spirit. Dickens considered *David Copperfield* his "favourite child."

Cohen's *künstler* is Lawrence Breavman, and Breavman strikes me as a Canadian version of Holden Caulfield, the teenage hero of J. D. Salinger's *The Catcher in the Rye*. Breavman's adolescence does not occupy the whole of the novel, but he is portrayed as a precocious youngster and an immature young adult, and to a large degree these sensibilities dominate. Both Breavman and Caulfield have a sharp eye for hypocrisy and phoniness. Although Breavman occasionally falters, as when he stuffs tissue paper into his shoes in order to appear taller, he redeems himself, laying the wads at Muffin's feet and demanding that she remove her own Kleenex prostheses. The main difference between them is that while Holden Caulfield is disenchanted (I think in particular of his disdain for motion pictures), Breavman believes in enchantment, sometimes in its most literal sense. One of the great comic sequences in our literature begins, "He read everything he could on hypnosis." Breavman walks through his neighbourhood inducing trance-like states in the dogs he encounters – that is to say, they fall asleep ("But was it natural sleep?"). Breavman believes that he can "make things happen." He is certain that he has caused Bertha's tumble from the tree, for instance, and the fight at the Palais D'Or. It is ironic that Breavman, again like Caulfield, "makes" almost nothing happen. Instead, he allows things to happen to him, and when they overwhelm him, he withdraws. His reaction to intimacy is flight, a behaviour he exhibits throughout the book, with Tamara, with Marshall. Then there is the year of employment at the brass foundary, which becomes a sort of hermitage.

Breavman has still more in common with the other great Salinger creation, Seymour Glass. Both characters are precocious children who become accomplished poets and search for spiritual enlightenment. Glass ends his life a suicide, but the difference is one of degree. Surely Breavman is due for major psychic trauma:

> One day what he did to her, to the child, would enter his understanding with such a smash of guilt that he would sit motionless for days, until others carried him and medical machines brought him back to speech.

Indeed, Breavman's similarities to both Caulfield and Glass point toward some remarkable connections between the two authors. Both of their fathers, for example, were in the garment industry. Salinger is, of course, the great recluse of North American literature; Cohen exhibits at least a tendency toward withdrawal, having spent time sequestered in a monastery. Most importantly, both writers are deeply concerned with spiritual enlightenment, and seek it in places far removed from their Jewish roots.

After *The Favourite Game*, Cohen published *Beautiful Losers* and then abandoned the novel form altogether, concentrating on poetry and songwriting. (I nevertheless consider *Death of a Lady's Man* a novel, and a very good one.) In his verse and yrics, he gives voice to many of the same themes that imbue *The Favourite Game*. One poem, "As the mist leaves no scar," serves as the novel's preface. The first stanza reads:

> As the mist leaves no scar
> On the dark green hill,
> So my body leaves no scar
> On you, nor ever will.

Scars are what the novel is all about: "Children show scars like medals. Lovers use them as secrets to reveal. A scar is what happens when the word is made flesh." The poem proclaims what would be for Breavman an idyllic relationship, a mixture of sensuality and spirituality that satisfies carnal desire yet has no dangerous physicality. One cannot help but think of the haunting refrain from Cohen's song "Suzanne": "She's touched your perfect body with her mind." In reality, though, two people cannot help but scar each other. Consider what happens when Shell sneaks up on Breavman as he composes: "He wheeled around in surprise, pencil in hand, and scraped skin from her cheek." Breavman's most satisfying relationship may well be with Lisa, the child; here we have the red string, the imaginary welts that can be lifted and vanished. Perfection lies in remaining untouched, yet the "favourite game" is, in fact, marring something unbroken: Bertha, the spinner, throws Breavman and his friends into freshly fallen snow.

Perfection has a particular significance for the writer. Breavman remembers "The stacks of exercise books dazzlingly empty of mistakes, more perfect than Perfect." It seems likely that Cohen decided to concentrate on songs (each of which he considers "a novel," as he has said so often) because in a song perfection seems tantalizingly possible. A novel is a large and cumbersome thing, susceptible to clutter and confusion. There are, however, few missteps in *The Favourite Game*, and Leonard Cohen sustains the highest level of poetic craftmanship throughout.

BY LEONARD COHEN

FICTION
The Favourite Game (1963)
Beautiful Losers (1966)

POETRY
Let Us Compare Mythologies (1956)
The Spice-Box of Earth (1961)
Flowers for Hitler (1964)
Parasites of Heaven (1966)
Selected Poems, 1956-1968 (1968)
The Energy of Slaves (1972)
Death of a Lady's Man (1978)
Book of Mercy (1984)
Stranger Music: Selected Poems and Songs (1993)